I0732738

Other work by Jorge Armenteros

Touch That Which We Cannot Possess
The Book of I

The Striped Tunic Trilogy
Air
The Roar of the River
The Spiral of Words

WE ARE NOT BUT WE ARE

Jorge Armenteros

SPUYTEN DUYVIL
NEW YORK CITY

© 2023 Jorge Armenteros
ISBN 978-1-959556-23-7
cover: Joseph Stella, American, born Italy, 1877–1946
Brooklyn Bridge 1919–20 Oil on canvas Yale University Art Gallery

Library of Congress Cataloging-in-Publication Data

Names: Armenteros, Jorge, author.
Title: We are not but we are / Jorge Armenteros.
Description: New York : Spuyten Duyvil, [2023]
Identifiers: LCCN 2023000497 | ISBN 9781959556237 (paperback)
Subjects: LCGFT: Fiction.
Classification: LCC PS3601.R5723 W4 2023 | DDC 813/.6--dc23/
eng/20230106
LC record available at https://lccn.loc.gov/2023000497

I had no wish to take any determined route on that stroll; I attempted, rather, a maximum latitude of probabilities in order not to wear out expectation with an obligatory anticipation of a single one of them. I was able, within the imperfect limits of possibility, to walk, as they say, at random. I accepted, without any conscious prejudice but that of avoiding the wider avenues and streets, the most obscure invitations of chance.

Jorge Luis Borges, *A Personal Anthology*

Part One:

THE CROSSING

Last time I saw him, his eyes were cascading, and there were no hands to collect them. The emptiness around him did not seem his own. He appeared improbable, unrelated as if he had landed inside such absence by accident. I tried to reach out to him with both of my hands. But my hands began to cascade into the same emptiness and no other hands were there to collect mine either. So, I closed my eyes and waited for the moon to race across the entire arc of the night. When the morning arrived and I opened my eyes, he was no longer there. I was alone, with both of my hands, lacking nonexistence. Why this memory now? Perhaps because reality mounts another attack on me. I can sense it: the undulating body of the earth below my feet, the push of the wind, the mineral smell of matter, the closeness of others. I shall close my eyes again.

Soon, the moment that will determine the rest of the moments contained within this day is bound to arrive. The inevitability of such a moment does not surprise me. This is how things ought to be. I feel a man holding onto my elbow and pulling me back from the edge of the sidewalk. He says that I should open my eyes if I intend to cross the street. He may be right, but at the same time, he may be wrong. Unbeknownst to him, his action changes everything. I do open my eyes and proceed with crossing the street. On the other side of the street, a certain reality waits for me.

From this instant, let chance dictate all the events that may take place during the day. The events, that is, because the trend of thoughts will likely evolve differently, not following chance per se, but probably the inner dictum of my unconscious. And since nobody can predict what the unconscious is secretly brewing, my day is nothing but mist about to clear. I do not fear this sentiment—to the contrary—let it sit next to me and sing me a berceuse.

This other side of the street already looks old, as if I left it behind years ago. The sidewalk and the buildings are recognizable, but they seem to have faded a little. However, since I just walked across the street, it is impossible for this other side to have changed much. Perhaps a new reality offers a different perspective. This, I could not have envisioned. How about the man who held my elbow? Clearly, he did not want me to get hurt. But was he protecting me from oncoming traffic or from this new reality?

Turning my back on the abandoned side of the street seems the appropriate thing to do. That forces me to walk into a narrow alley at the end of which a small plaza opens up. The mature trees stand relatively straight and provide a delicious shade. A burnt-gold bench, tired of people, does not react when I sit on it. On the bench, under the green shade of the trees, I come to the realization that my perspective has not changed enough. What I see in front of me is in constant transformation, but the way I see all of it is the same. However, that would imply that I cannot change at all—an uncomfortable thought, even unbearable. So, once again, I close my eyes. This time there is no apparent danger. Well, my eyelids could melt and fuse with my eyes. Since this vast new reality is unknown to me, that may be a valid possibility. It would also be possible to eradicate time. But I do not want so many misfortunes for myself. I take a deep breath and allow the old ships of my mind to part the waters.

In one of those ships, I sailed to my place of origin. Not recognizing the land or its people, I doubted I was really born there. Then came an old woman who called me by my name. She asked me where I had been, what marvelous things my eyes had seen. Without credible answers to offer, I felt the need to invent a story that would gratify her curiosity. I spoke of subterranean time, of deep reaches, of drums and lances, of broken springs and streams, of the flight of the eagle, of oblique cities and taciturn horizons. She followed every word of the story and attributed her private emotional twist to what she heard. Satisfied with the prodigious experience, she thanked me. She then invoked my name once more and begged me to part again in search of more adventures. Disarmed, I boarded the ship and abandoned my unrecognizable place of origin.

Two minutes or two centuries later, I open my eyes. A young girl has come to sit next to me on the bench. She seems calm as if endowed with old wisdom. Instead of holding a doll in her arms, she is holding a cat. To my surprise, the cat remains in a placid and meditative state in her arms. It does not bolt away savagely as most cats tend to do. Maybe the girl has unexpected instincts. I ask her for her name. My question floats unattended in the air for a while. The girl seems to be considering whether to answer or not. She then turns toward me and offers me a pure and radiant smile. The entire girl is contained in that smile. Her name, her short history, her dreams of what tomorrow will bring, her love for the cat—all her sentiments encapsulated in a single honest expression. I smile back at her, but I can barely communicate as much, the years of questioning everything having jaded any original purity. With ease, she gets off the bench and walks away from the plaza. The cat follows behind her, wiggling and un-wiggling its tail.

I understand there were one thousand and one nights when incomplete stories were told, and promises were made. I do not count with time as ample as that, nor do I want to enter into the realm of fiction. I must, therefore, handle this new reality as if it were as real as the one across the street. But, the only problem is that nobody will corroborate this reality as different from the previous one. Crossing the street changed the momentum of the day, but did it change anything more substantial? I will refrain from answering that question. For the moment, I will allow for the frigid lake waters to flood my consciousness. A blue numbness then soothes me.

Upon the urge to continue with my day, I decide to leave the plaza and enter the rest of the world. The grand world cannot help but to exist out there in anticipation. People need to engage with this grand world in order for the world to find its reason to exist. It is not up to people to find their meaning in this grand world, but for the world itself to realize its purpose in relation to us. I have waited many years for such delivery. Nothing, nothing at all. Nevertheless, I will venture into the belly of the beast and find my nest.

A certain familiarity surrounds me: the houses, the people, the street corners, the smell of mankind, the arrogance of the sky. Further into this realm, I begin to wonder if this is nothing but a simulacrum of everything I have experienced before. How would I know the difference? How could I tell apart two competing and identical realities? This, I cannot solve at this moment. So, accepting this yellow impotence, I continue my march like the waters of a river.

After a short while, I find myself standing in front of a house that looks like my house. This could very well be my house. I may even live in this house. Nothing seems odd about it. There is the gate at the entrance, the short path leading to the porch, the door with the number "3" nailed on its forehead, and the rest of the house behind it. Flawlessly, as I have done thousands of times, I find myself opening the door and letting myself into this house.

Inside the comfort of the house, I must confront my future actions. I can behave as I have always behaved, following known routines based on pre-established reasoning. If I respect the arrow of time, this privileged moment would be my present. But if I were to break that arrow and ignore the path that led me here, considering that in the process, time is simply a given, then the future would be as determined or undetermined as the past. I could then choose a new path going forward. Uncertain as to how to proceed, I regard the chair by the window that looks as inviting as it always has.

What I find surprising and reassuring at the same time is to find a bottle of my favorite red wine in the kitchen. I serve myself a glass and come to sit in the chair by the window. From this vantage point, I can observe the swallows oscillating at a low altitude. Their flight is circular. They are wise, the swallows. I decide not to decide anything at this point. Sitting here and watching the birds should suffice. If this is a fulcrum in the continuum of my life; then, I should be still, risk nothing, and remain calm. Even lifting my arm to bring the glass of wine to my lips should be done with care. Yes, the body is simple to control; the mind, however, is a restless beast.

Outside of the window, life happens as it should. Trees build their long, unwavering future, grass grows in desperation, insects live their trivial lives, children play without knowing, and I am witness to the spectacle. This scenery does not challenge my concept of reality. A previous reality could have contained all of these scenes. Thus, I wonder if the fact that these scenes are recognizable renders them obsolete and useless. In other words, should a new reality contain nothing but unedited experiences? I look out of the window again and try to see everything as if new. Nothing at all; not in the first take. But as I take a second look, I am assaulted by the image of an old man who comes to stand just outside the gate to my house. He carries nothing with him, just an obvious emptiness. He does not ring the bell, for which I am grateful since I am not certain I want to meet him. If I want to usher this new reality without pre-imposed obligations, I should be free to invite this man into this house; but at the same time, I should be free to ignore him completely. Both options should be acceptable.

The problem again resides within the mind, where arbitrary thoughts lead us to act in arbitrary ways. But who am I to judge what is or is not arbitrary? I set the glass of wine on the floor next to the chair and make my way to the gate of the house. When I open the gate, the old man steps inside at once and greets me as if I were an old friend. I ask him to come inside the house, and he does. I pull another chair and set it next to the one I was occupying. Then we both sit down and look out the window. My reality has not changed much. I am still sitting in the same chair, contemplating what happens in the outside world as framed by the window. The only change is that there is now an old man sitting next to me. In the interest of symmetry, I ask the old man if he cares for a glass of wine. He says that he cares not for wine, but that perhaps wine cares for him. Understanding that he is completely correct in his assessment, I get up and pour him a glass of wine. Once in my chair again, I raise my glass and toast to chance. The old man toasts to the vicissitudes of time. Then we both look at the leaves on the trees as they flutter nervously.

Could this house, with its breathing walls, its flowing corridors, its hugging roof, its eyes out to the world, be his house and not mine? Perhaps it should have been him opening the door to a stranger. He seems at peace with himself, in this house, drinking my wine. If the wine cares for him, as he mentioned, maybe they are already acquainted with each other. The purpose of his visit may be no other than a return to his home. I could ask him if, indeed, he feels at home in this house. I could ask many questions, but perhaps it is better to ask none. Not knowing is grander than knowing, for it allows everything. In this spirit of uncertainty, I remain contemplating the world outside and the old man inside.

Once he finishes the glass of wine, the old man closes his eyes and seems to fall asleep. Instead of beginning to snore, he begins to talk. He says that the world outside has not changed much since he last regarded it. He says that the wine has not changed in character since he last tasted it. He also says that I have not changed much, even though he is not sure he has ever seen me before. He then gets up from the chair and prepares to leave. At the gate of the house, he thanks me profusely for my understanding. When I ask him where he is going, he says he needs to cross the street to figure that out.

#

Apart from the window and the world of outside images, there is a world of sounds inside this house. The walls whisper, and I cannot contain myself from attempting to decipher what they say. I hold my breath and continue to exist in absolute silence while I listen. The whispers grow in volume but remain unintelligible. The walls may be reflecting layer upon layer of conversations that have taken place inside this house. Secrets may be revealed; promises offered, maybe a lament never heard by anyone. I place my ear against one of the walls and hear my name as if someone was calling me from far away. Perhaps what I hear is not my name, but my desire that someone would call me. Desires must elicit sounds. For what other reason would the wind exist if not to disperse those sounds?

A lamp, bathing in its own light, hums a simple melody in the corner of the salon. In its simplicity, the melody seems familiar to me. I must have heard it before. The melody of light must be part of every house where there is a lamp in a corner. Because of its universal character, then, the familiar melody does not make this house any more personal than before. My steps on the floor do sound rather personal. When I stop walking, I do not hear my steps. When I walk, I only hear my steps and my steps only. There is no echo, no mysterious reverberations.

Then I hear a heart pumping blood through veins and arteries. The pulse has a human rhythm, the cadence of life considered from within. Nothing indicates impending anguish, nor ecstasy. It sounds like a heart sustaining a life in harmony. I better be careful about this sound, for there is harmony in death, precisely when nothing is bound to chance anymore. But this is a beating heart, full of life. This house must have a heart. And of all the noises it contains, the sound of its heart should be the most soothing. I must be hearing its beating now. Or is it my heart that I hear? Are they different?

As I continue to meander through corridors and rooms, I begin to wonder if there could be real silence inside this house. I do not mean complete lack of noise, for that, in itself, is a sort of noise. Silence of the mind is what I wonder about—the one that can be attained in the midst of brutal noise—the one that resembles nothingness. Evidently, silence has not come my way since I crossed the street. I have not searched for silence specifically. Instead, I have dealt with concerns as they materialize unannounced. Upon consideration, silence seems rather fluid. It cannot be completely captured, nor retained. Even in the middle of a still night, when the moist air drops on your skin, up in the dark sky the moon howls. We do not necessarily hear the moon, but the vision of the white body advancing through the stillness implies a sound, and we hear it even when we do not hear it. The mind yearns for silence, but noise gets in the way. Universally, physically, and spiritually, noise enters our consciousness.

I attempt to cover my ears, but instead of silence, what I hear is the muted sound of blood, or perhaps the flow of my thoughts. I am not sure which. But certainly not the absence of noise. Maybe that is what life sounds like: the continuous hum of cells churning chemical processes or the unending birthing of ideas inside our mind. Life could also sound like foreign words spoken or sung, inaccessible to us, but somehow entirely explicit due to the inherent emotion in their sound or rhythm. That ought to be the purest form of communication when the meaning is inherent in the sound of the language. A man speaks and what he says is clear and deeply felt. A woman speaks, and what she says moves the universe. These experiences occur even when the words are not completely understood. But their sound has conveyed all possible meanings. That ought to be the sound of language.

To immerse myself in the realm of sounds brings me great pleasure, especially when the sounds are musical notes. Those notes are capable of eliciting emotions in a split second. Those weightless and incorporeal notes exist thanks to the invisible and ubiquitous air. How brilliant, everything out of nothing. Music has been performed in this house. I can tell, even if I cannot hear traces at this moment. However, when the sound of my steps bounces against the walls, it returns to my ears with a certain syncopated rhythm. The sound of my steps could not attain such cadence without the spirit of music intervening somehow. Perhaps the sound gets laced with old musical notes embedded in the walls. I cannot recognize the melody, but it makes me think of the ocean.

The doorbell then rings, not music, but the sound of an announcement. Considering that I may, or may not, know the person at the door, I hesitate a bit before answering. If this were my house, I would probably know who is ringing the bell at this moment. I could even be expecting the person's arrival. This is a comforting thought. However, it is entirely possible for the person at the door to be a total stranger. On the other hand, if this were not my house, there would be no possibility for me to anticipate who is at the door right now. This is an uncomfortable thought. The doorbell rings again. I retrieve my steps through corridors and rooms until I reach the door. Here I pause. I could let myself out of the house, cross the path, and make it to the gate. Then I will encounter he or she who has announced him or herself. That will be a pivotal moment because the recognition of the person, or lack thereof, will be consummated. The doorbell rings once more. I let myself out of the house, and immediately the sounds of the world assault me. I cross the path and reach the gate to the street. I open the gate.

There are times when what we anticipate is exactly what takes place. Like the sun rising in the morning or ourselves getting old with the years. But there are other times when life deals irregular cards. And that is the sensation I get when I find myself at the gate face-to-face with Babylos, my friend from childhood. I feel like crying, but at the same time, I feel like running away. Babylos seems to welcome the encounter because he does not cry, nor does he run away. When I ask him how long it took him to find me, he says that he was not looking for me, that he felt like ringing the bell because of the number "3" at the door. He goes on to explain that the number "3" is his lucky number. I do feel a certain affinity toward the number "3," but I will not share that with him now. I remember the uncertain hours of sunlight when, as children, we were so afraid. There were moments when the sweetness of danger may have altered what went on to happen in our lives without us never knowing.

Babylos was as tall as he was slender, also hunched over, and none of that has changed. He asks me to accompany him for a short walk without giving any reason for the request. My heart skips a beat and then starts racing. I know I may be about to lose some of my eternity. But this fear burns white, it carries no heat, nor does it lead to anguish. Perhaps the expectation of what never happened is as soft as a ghost, as white. Down the street, we walk for a while. He seems to know exactly where he is going; he does not vacillate. So, I follow him trusting this territory is known to him. I recognize most of the houses as if I have lived here for a long time, which is entirely possible. Eventually, we come to stand in front of a house surrounded by a fence. Inside the fence, in a wall-manicured patio, a lemon tree grows in its full citrus glory. The yellow starry tree plays with the wind right in front of us, unabashed.

Then Babylos begins pacing back and forth as if throbbing with pain. He does not say a word, but he seems to be containing an explosion inside of him. When I get a glimpse of his face, I see it has mutated. The eyes have fallen inside, and the mouth is darker. He could be remembering what he does not want to remember. The body follows the mind, especially when the mind is bitten by a certain darkness. Babylos says that all the little suns in the tree are for the taking. That all we need to do is jump over the fence and serve ourselves. When I do not respond to his suggestion, his pacing accelerates even more, making it uncomfortable for me to watch. Then taking advantage of his height, he climbs over the fence in two seconds. Once inside the patio, he begins to ransack the lemon tree. He picks as many lemons as he can. He stuffs them in his pockets, inside his jacket. He starts chewing on them as if they were apples. And the carnage continues until the lemon tree is entirely desecrated; until no little sun is left to shine.

I should question the reality of this moment. Are these only reflections upon a surface that is no longer mine? Was I the one meant to jump over the fence? Will there be other trees, other lives? Regardless of the impossible answers, I remain still until Babylos jumps over the fence once more and comes to my side. He is calmer now, even serene. But his face is still hollow, dragged inside. There may be a bridge spanning the void between the two of us. But I cannot see it. Slowly, now, he turns away from me and continues to walk down the street. He leaves me here, standing alone. I wonder what thoughts are rushing through his mind.

#

The street that I crossed earlier today must be nearby. If this is my neighbor, and everything seems to indicate it is, I should be able to reach the street by making two consecutive right turns and then walking straight for three more blocks. Nothing known should stand on my way. I proceed on my quest for the divisive street and make the first required right turn. When I am about to make the second right turn, I realize that I left the gate to the house completely open. Anyone, friend or foe, could just walk into the house and do as they wish. And since I cannot fathom what anyone's wishes could possibly be, I veer like a wind on the high seas and head back to the house.

There is a certain leadenness to my steps. Even though I want to reach the house as soon as possible, I walk as if I never wanted to get there. My feet move, but there is no ground below them. And instead of advancing, I begin to fall. Deep into myself, I fall. How deep I cannot tell. Above me, the surface of a lake covers the sky. There is sufficient light under the surface and no noise at all. And I feel at once relief and wonderment, for never in my life have I fallen into a place as strange and as silent as this. I am not concerned about breathing; why take on that obligation now? Whether time moves on is another useless question right now. As to the reason for having fallen, all I can say is that it happened. Outside of time, there are no memories. I can attest to that, for I cannot remember what I was doing before I fell. But, did I fall, or have I been here all along?

All of a sudden, I part the waters above me while a certain springiness returns to my steps. Even though I am relatively close to the house, I hasten to get there. As I get near, I see at once that the gate is effectively open. I stop in my tracks and survey the surroundings. There is nobody around at this time. The air carries itself with indifference, as if not wanting to be a witness. Slowly, I proceed through the open gate. Nothing indicates that anyone has entered in my absence. I follow the path until the front door. All quiet here. Through the door, I go with apprehension. Nobody.

I have returned to this house as if it were mine. That would imply having had a past in this place and a sense of possession. That would also require me to be the same person who left the house not too long ago to answer the doorbell to encounter no other than unexpected Babylos. He, who was not really looking for me. Or was he? I get a sense that there is a beginning to everything that has happened today. But, at what point does anything start? Does the sea begin at the shore, or is it at the shore that it ends?

The house is now resting. It cares not for what I do or think. It simply abandons itself to an afternoon nap. I can feel a gentle breeze come in through the windows when the house takes a deep breath. I can also hear the slowing heartbeat. What a large heart this is. The natural rhythms of life invite me to settle down and worry less. I accept the placid cradle and let go of my disquiet. I float a little. A legion of memories begins to march through my mind. They advance in no particular order. There is me as a child, before knowing that later in life, I would not remember my childhood. There are all the departures, voluntary and otherwise. And the faces that looked at my face, now with the eyes closed. And I can barely recognize much more. A slow march this is, not nefarious, but not celebratory either. Strangely, there are no memories of this house. Even though we now breathe the same air and hear each other's hearts, even though I identify with its walls and its windows, this house does not reveal itself in my memories.

The inanimate objects scattered through the house do not reveal much either. I would have ignored them even if they served a purpose. Perhaps that lack of attachment interferes with my recognition. But what is the point in recognizing an object? The feelings are the ones that matter as they are the true fabric of life. However, I could have lived here an entire life without truly feeling much. This is an uncomfortable thought, but I am holding onto it for an instant. If all the accumulated experiences had no particular emotional essence; then, I should have the right to remember nothing—a rather liberating concept that is. Life, then, could take a new, free, and unencumbered course. Without memories, there could be no expectations. And without expectations, there could be no deceptions. The recipe for a placid life would be to have no feelings—another uncomfortable thought.

At this point, the house starts coughing, and the suspended spell comes crashing to the floor. All the memories flee from my mind, and I find myself, once again, looking out the window. We look outside when looking inside burns like a white flame. Outside, in the open air, nothing ever stays the same. What I saw earlier today has already metamorphosed into what I am seeing this moment. The air is not the same air as the river is never the same river. The directives of these transformations are unknown to me. I accept them, even when I cannot name them. Regardless, I continue to contemplate the world through the window in expectation of any sign that would help me decipher the reality of this moment. I am patient, but I am not eternal. So, I will rest here, like a cactus hoping to flower.

The problem with expecting is that one may grow roots. And once the roots take hold of the ground under our feet, we risk immobility. The entangled earth will never fall off from below our feet. The only way to extricate ourselves would be by taking a hatchet to our roots. Even if liberating, a painful operation that would be. Better not to grow roots at this moment when so much uncertainty is in the air. I detach myself from the window and the view to the outside. I confirm that no roots are growing from the sole of my shoes. Relieved, then, I decide to interact with this new reality on my terms. I will face any and all events that intersect with my path, but I will be the one initiating the original motion. Resolved, I exit the house and come to stand outside of the gate, unconditionally exposed to the vagaries of this irregular life.

Seen from this perspective, the street has very little to offer. There is asphalt, a sidewalk, a few feeble trees, insipid houses. The sky is actually more interesting for it is not grounded; it can change its temper on a whim like the ancient Greek gods. But if I were to move in this earthly realm, I would have to pay close attention to what surrounds me and not the sky above. Perhaps true changes will arrive as a result of my own actions in the immediacy of my body. If I move my hands, something is bound to happen. If I have a thought, and then as a result of that thought, I move my hands or my legs, something is bound to happen again. This time, however, it would be the mind that originated everything. I imagine the world would change as a result of my actions, regardless of what originated them. To test the various possibilities, I decide to extend my arm in a straight angle and open my hand. Having pierced the universe with my hand, I simply wait for a response.

A young woman shakes my hand and says she is very happy to see me. She seems so honest that I believe what she says, even if I do not recognize her. With her short hair and simple eyes, she could be my neighbor from across the street. But I cannot recall ever talking to her, even when her short hair and simple eyes are quite endearing to me. She stands right in front of me, smiling, but not saying another word. A universe of possibilities explodes inside my mind. I can say hello to her and withdraw back into the house. I can ask where she is heading to confirm whether she is my neighbor or not. I could invite her to take a walk with me. I could also close my eyes and pretend none of this is happening right now. I could do any one of those things and many more, but there will be a consequence. Like there is a consequence when we look straight at the sun.

I let go of her hand, and forests come down crashing in their somber greenness. Not holding her hand is akin to not possessing her. But I have never possessed such a forest. Letting go, then, is a clean breath and a silent desire. She does not say her name, nor does she ask for mine. She simply collects her hand and continues to walk down the street as if going somewhere. Her silhouette shrinks with every one of her steps until there is nothing visual left of her. In my mind, however, she remains.

Since she could be an essential part of my future, I resolve to follow her trace. She could be as unimportant as stale bread, but she could also be the center of a universe I have yet to know. Standing here in passive contemplation will not change anything. Likewise, if I were to go after her and actually find her, she may turn out to be nothing but a void. Uncertainty comes to greet me again, but this time I will try to scurry away.

Down the street, I walk in the direction of her disappearance. What I follow is only the memory of having seen her, for no other sign of her presence can be found. There is a certain joy in pursuing her. It allows me to feel as if I were a deciding element in what is to come. My pursuit would be creating a past to look back into if I were to succeed in finding her. How fulfilling that would be! I search for her without knowing what I am looking for, but I am determined to search. With its fa-

miliar face, the street seems to welcome my steps. I am
not confronted with anything unknown, nor do I face a
total recognition of trees, sidewalks, and dogs. I move
with ease, unafraid, prepared for what will come next.

I have searched before; when I was convinced about
the linearity of time, the laws of cause and effect, the
power of regularity. But searching today has a different
feeling. I feel as if I were floating over an immense and
accepting body of water—a river perhaps, or the ocean.
And I flow toward the image of the young woman without really knowing where she could be. But without a
rudder, I cannot point my body in any given direction.
It seems as if the waters take me where they will. I could
try to swim and fight the gentle current, but for what
purpose? Wouldn't she be floating just as I am? The
same body of water, with the same current, would bring
us both to a natural encounter. If, indeed, I am being
brought to her by the current, then I would not be ac-
tively searching for her. As a passive and contemplative
self, the outcome could even be a random one. And if I
were not a deciding element, I would not be creating a
past to refer to.

I allow for the natural passage of time to determine
the duration of my floating. I turn around streets, cross
a park where children are playing, and watch the people come and go from their homes. I remain alert and
calm at the same time while looking for any trace of the
young woman. But nothing around me conjures her im-

age again. Where she went may be part of her circle of fate, or perhaps it is my circle the fateful one. The waters that hold me begin to recede. Gently, I come to rest on my back on a street as common as any other. I find myself in a place I did not choose, aware that I was not the agent of this moment in my life. I intended to intervene in the course of the universe, but it seems the universe has a course of its own.

I wait for dryness; I wait for my body to feel as if new, unencumbered by the need to unravel any mystery. And once the sense of newness reveals itself supreme, I know I can forge ahead; ahead of a situation that begs understanding, or at a minimum, basic clarity. Therefore, I walk in the direction that seems most appropriate, toward the street that I crossed not too long ago, which ushered this sense of otherness. I recognize that I crossed a street and my sense of reality changed dramatically. I also recognize that such a sense of otherness may be due to a lack of recognition. So, what I really need to do at this point is to approach that same street and come to terms with its proposition. Not that a street by itself can propose much, but my response to whatever intersected my life as I crossed that street was wondrous.

#

The place cannot be far from here, physically. Since I crossed that street, I have only moved by foot. Not feeling any sense of exhaustion leads me to believe I could not have walked for too long. Mentally, I feel I have traversed an epoch; but that is a different matter. At this point, I am moving over land with my own two feet. Not knowing exactly in what direction to walk is rather liberating. All I have to do is follow my instincts. Surprisingly, people I come across behave so gently; they allow plenty of room for me to walk with ease. Even the air seems encouraging by pushing me ahead with a fresh touch. It may take two minutes to arrive at the street, or it may take two centuries. It does not matter, for the process of walking unencumbered is in itself an achievement. I have walked great distances before over so many years. But not until this moment have I felt so at ease while walking. Even though the neighborhood seems so familiar, it still feels different, lighter. I could consider everything I am going through as known experiences, but they just do not feel the same. Perhaps everything has already existed this way without me noticing. Or perhaps we are unaware of the parallel lives we live.

After a while, my steps bring me to a fork in the road. This situation forces me to make a choice and decide between the two paths. Therefore, I have to engage my mind in the process of walking, effectively ending my freedom from encumbrance. No matter which path I follow, I will be aware that I ignored the other one, and that is enough to engage the mind for a while. If I am to continue walking unencumbered, I need to believe that the two paths are identical, that choosing one path over the other would make no difference at all. Alternatively, I can think that the paths are completely different, but that their outcomes will be the same. But perhaps, more interestingly, I can choose one path at this moment and be completely satisfied with my choice, knowing that in my parallel life, I will certainly choose the other path at some other moment in time. In that case, both possibilities would be explored, so there would be no need to make a conscious choice now. And that is exactly what I do. For this life of mine, and at this moment, I chose the path heading left.

Slowly, then, I continue my march. I do not need to tell anyone of my imminent arrival, for I am walking only for myself. I am the only one who could stop me, and I am the only one who could propel myself forward. When looking for answers that pertain to the self, we are utterly alone. The street I search may not contain any answers; it may be just a threshold, a marker, or the mythical line in the sand. But it does exist, even if the meaning of having crossed it flies away like a winged hope.

As I advance, I notice that the sound of my steps generates an echo. I clearly hear the one-two-one-two of my steps against the sidewalk, but I also hear a three-four-three-four coming from somewhere around me. Anyone could be walking beside me, behind me, or even ahead of me. Could anyone be following me? Why would anyone be interested in following me? To try to ascertain what is happening, I come to a full stop. There is complete silence, or close to it. I fail to hear the one-two or the three-four anymore. I scan the sidewalk in all directions and confirm that there is nobody around. I do feel, however, as if the air has become heavier. The moment I resume my walk, the two sets of steps can be heard again at the same rhythm. Once more, I stop, and so do the sound of my steps and the echo. Why would there be an echo? I am not walking in a closed chamber. Maybe what I hear are my own steps after having turned right instead of left at the fork. Maybe, for the first time, I am aware of a parallel life.

Regardless of what happens alongside my current life, I continue to walk until I get a glimpse of the street I am looking for. It grows in the distance like a dark canyon. As I get closer, I find not a street but a deep wound on the surface of the earth, and I look into it—an essentially harrowing and unsettling view. I wonder if everyone who crosses this street feels the same way if they endure a shift as dislodging as mine. Even if I fail to understand why I crossed the street, I will no longer look at that wound. So, I turn around and walk away.

The air releases its grip on the starkness of the moment and assumes a gentler flow. My steps become lighter and seem to have silenced any distracting echo. The neighborhood, however, continues to appear familiar and unfamiliar at the same time. I believe this is the life that I am living. Why would I have any doubts? I believe I am heading back to my house. I believe what will happen in my house will happen to me. Even if I hear the steps of an alternate life, the one I have right in front of me is my own. How it all comes to happen, I am not certain. How much control I have over what happens is even more uncertain. And after looking down into that void separating territories of seemingly continuous existences, I would not venture to guess how it all comes about.

Should I try to continue with my old life? Should I start a different life in this new reality? Is this indeed a new reality, or has it always existed alongside the one I am familiar with? None of that would matter unless I were aware that the possibility of a parallel life existed. And that is precisely the problem, that after crossing that street, I cannot define myself exactly as I used to. But how would I have defined myself in the past? I know that I am a man. But I also know that I am tired of being a man. However, I am not tired of dreaming. In this potentially new existence, I would go on dreaming. Yes, I have had many misfortunes I would not like to forget; otherwise, I would have to endure them again. I must be careful because things return to their place, but if the place itself has shifted, everything would fall in disarray. Much chaos would ensue. So, I need to think about myself as a different person from the one I used to know, although closely allied to it. The familiarity would allow for continuity while preventing a catastrophic schism. But how many degrees of separation am I ready to tolerate? A moot question that is, for I suppose that will be determined as I carry on.

Once more, I venture toward the house that seems to be my house. It occurs to me, however, that before entering that house again and reassuming a modicum of fresh existence, I should come to terms with the existence that predated this one. I refuse to accept that this present follows a determined past, nor that the future is determined in any fashion. But revisiting what I know about myself could be revealing—and revolting. I was never a slave nor a conqueror. I think I was a free man. Free in the legal sense, for we are always prisoners of our innermost fears and wishes. I must have been happy, sometimes. I made a living by playing the flute. Indeed, I convinced the air to vibrate in harmonious ways to conjure what people call music. The sound I produced did not belong to me, nor to the audience. It simply existed, invisible and insubstantial, but nonetheless captivating. That musical sound was recorded, the only proof of its existence. But that recorded existence is nothing other than a sound, once again invisible and insubstantial. How I became a flute player is unclear to me, for I have forgotten so much. Perhaps I made a decision resulting in my becoming a flute player. The inner workings of such a decision, however, are now a mystery to me. Would the currents of my reasoning flow in a similar way in the future? A fanciful thought.

I am alone now. I notice this condition not because I sense an absence, but because I feel like a person walking alone. My steps do not synchronize with anyone's steps. I move freely, unfastened. Did I always walk alone? Unclear, because at this very moment, I would not mind coming across the young woman with short hair and simple eyes that shook my hand not too long ago. Her reality intersected with mine, it quickly vanished, but I was enchanted. I must have experienced fortuitous encounters like that one in the past. Or perhaps it was not as fortuitous; it could have been one in the chain of many. I do not want to be a solitary ghost blowing my flute by the sea. I do not want to traverse a thousand years of air, months, weeks of air, my footsteps polishing the lonely sidewalk.

My body casts a shadow on the sidewalk ahead of me. I walk toward the shadow as the shadow walks away from me. The dark silhouette responds to my movements like a soul. It is not merely the absence of light created by my body blocking the sun, but the very essence of who I am at this moment. The shadow is not my other, for we are one and the same. I accept it; I integrate its existence into mine. But the shadow moves ahead of me in space, if not in time. Following the steps of my shadow, I continue to advance until I come to stand in front of my uncertain house. I consider that I may be a shadow of what I was before, on the other side of that street. I may be the light and its absence, at once myself, and what I have been.

#

The house seems content to hear me as I enter through the door, as I walk through its corridors. Its lungs expand, taking in the air my body sheds. The walls seem to glow, and a curtain at the window flaps with abandon. The house may recognize me, or like a street cat, it is just happy that someone comes by. I wonder if there are relics of my life lying around in this house. Objects or memories, or maybe an old pain. I could rummage through every room in search of physical connections that may shed light on my existence. But in so doing, I may unearth layers of discomfort. This shall be a quiet moment, better not upset an unknown universe.

I will refrain from exploring the details inherent in the numerous objects that populate this house. Music, however, escapes this self-imposed rule. The sound of music pertains to no specific time nor a particular place; that sound is not bound to this world like material objects are. Music rather behaves like the human mind: intangible, but emotional at its core. I feel free to listen to the hum of this house. I relax, and I listen. And soon, my ears detect a melody that resonates with the sound of my life thus far. I cannot tell its origin, but the melody carries me back to moments I have forgotten, and at the same time, projects me forward to moments I have yet to experience. It seems to float inside of me, like blood. I move around the house to find its source, and everywhere I turn to, the melody is already there. It seems to be oozing from the bones of the house.

While searching inside a closet, to my surprise, I find a flute similar to the one I used to play. I hesitate before playing it, for it may sound just like I expect it to sound. And if that were the case, how could I explain the existence of this flute in this house? Nevertheless, I venture to blow into the flute. And the simple wooden flute makes a sweet, simple sound—as I imagined, and as I feared. Yes, it is the same sound I have produced before from a flute identical to this one. That leads me to consider that the same person who played the original flute is the one playing this flute right now—that is, two distinct flutes but only one player. Another possible alternative to consider would be that there is only one flute which I played before and that the same flute is now being played by my shadow. But this is not the time for questions—this is the time for music. Thus, I let the air flow through my lungs, through the wooden body of the flute, through the spaces contained within the walls of the house, through my ears where it is transformed into a neural signal, and through my mind where the music tries to speak to me. I continue to blow and let the flute say what it has to. I recognize this is not my song, but the song the flute needs to sing.

The flute swallows the air and transforms it into a soothing sound the house seems to appreciate. The walls assume a softer tonality and lean against each other. They rest, they murmur softly among themselves. The roof arches its back and settles in a comfortable position. The trees and the flowers in the yard look inside the house through the open windows. They also listen. I simply allow myself to exist in the midst of this little miracle until the flute exhausts itself out. Nothing can be as pure and boundless as the voice of the instruments. Satisfied, I set the flute aside, knowing that in case I lose my way, a connection to this pure universe is at arm's reach.

If this house has contained me, it must be a witness to what I have been. This house could be a dwelling that has embraced my fears, my joys, my defeats. A silent witness that is, for I would not expect it to divulge anything to anybody, myself included. I am ready to accept it as my home in this new reality. I do not expect any special considerations from its part. If I were about to repeat a mistake, the house could not warn me against it. Neither could the house point me in the direction of happiness. I have to accept it as I would accept an old friend that has lost his tongue. What I will never know, however, is if the house is content with having me inside its walls.

What if the house is weary of my physical presence, my thoughts, my dreams? It may be looking forward to a new reality of its own, unrelated to mine. I know the house is accepting of the music, I just confirmed that. But the music is pure, and I cannot say the same thing about myself.

I think I have the freedom to choose. At least in appearance. I chose to cross the street, and I chose to continue walking without turning back. When I stood in front of this house, I chose to come inside. I have interacted with this uncertain world with certainty. But that does not guarantee that I am shaping my reality in any one form or another. I could be just as impotent as this house, waiting to see who walks through my door, hoping for soothing music to reach my ears. I could be a dwelling to my emotions without the capacity to alter them. Like a house, I could also be forgotten, abandoned, torn down. Perhaps nobody lives inside of me, and thus, the sense of otherness I feel when I look inside. Maybe all we have is a void that no universe can fill. But I still need a house, both outside and inside of myself.

Were anyone to ask me what forces led me to cross the street, I would have to say, "It so happens." Upon revisiting the moments that just preceded the crossing, my memory can only reveal a few wingless butterflies. Maybe a sense of impotence pushed me, maybe a dry air. We are led to believe that everything happens for a reason. If so, a clear trajectory comprising thoughts and events would have brought me to the verge of the crossing. Maybe there was a crisis, a revolt, a fall from a pedestal. But all I can summon is a vision of nothingness. An entire life, worthy or not, coalesced at that point when the crossing began, and then came what happened after the crossing, which is exactly what I am doing this moment—nothing other than wondering what happened before the crossing.

Perhaps the problem lies in thinking that this new existence is happening at a time after the crossing, that somehow my life on the other side of the street pertains to the past. Yes, I do have a memory of being a flute player, and that memory may imply a temporal relation toward the current moment. But what if that memory is not a memory at all but a recognition? I can postulate: "Here is a flute, and I can play it; therefore, I was a flute player." Conversely, I could say: "Here is a flute, and I can play it; therefore, I will become a flute player." The arrow of time can travel in both directions. Maybe I am returning to where I have always been, on this side of the street, the one that seems so unfamiliar to me.

To take a breath of fresh air and to lighten my thoughts, I decide to step out of the house and contemplate the world as it spins on its axis. Out on the sidewalk, I can hear the breathing of the world, and the continual breathing of the world is what we call silence. At this time of the day, the silence is magnificent, uninterrupted. A pure light comes to touch my face, and I allow it. It seems to remember me, this light, as if the gesture of touching my face is an ancient one. But I know that light cares not for time, so the touch is as fresh as it is gentle. This comforts me, for I need to feel anew. I resolve to restrain my thoughts from setting up a stage, from playing out the theater of the world. What I need now is to come to terms with nothing, to learn to exist out of time. I do not want this existence to exist me. I could let myself be carried away by whatever happens within the silence of the world. I am ready to take the risk of chance.

#

On the sidewalk, sleeping, or simply bored with its inanimate way of life, a gray pebble rests on its back. Or perhaps it rests on its belly—I would not know the difference. This pebble is alone, as no others of its kind are gathered around. I would imagine that similar to me; this pebble is not sure how it got to be here, in this very place, at this very moment. Most likely, the pebble does not care. I do care to know how I got here, but I am not entertaining those thoughts now. On its own, the pebble will not make a move. It would rest there until the end of the world unless the world decides to interact with it. This pebble is eternal.

I could not rest like the pebble, placid in its eternal dream. I need to interact with my surroundings in an effort to find meaning. I decide, then, to intertwine my destiny with that of the pebble. So, with a modicum of force, I kick the pebble square on its chest. The pebble flies for two or three meters before landing on its head and rolling down the sidewalk. It hits the front wall of a house, bounces a few more times, and finally comes to a full stop. The path it took was random. Yes, I set it into motion but without knowing the distance it would travel, the trajectory, the number of bounces, or the final spot where it would come to lie. The pebble is resting now as it did a few seconds ago, completely unaware of what happened before and ready to rest there forever. This pebble exudes blissfulness.

I make my way to where the pebble is waiting for me. I kneel down to observe it at a close distance. It is unscathed; it is intact; it is perfect. Deciding to try my luck again, I kick the pebble once more with whatever imprecision my foot would impart. This time the pebble takes a longer flight. It travels over a well-manicured yard and eventually falls in the street gutter far away from where I stand. I can barely see it there among the rubbish. If my destiny will become intertwined with that of the pebble, the fact that it is lying in the gutter is unflattering. I run to its rescue, or perhaps to my rescue. However, I come to realize that I will not be capable of kicking the pebble in any one particular direction. No matter how hard I try, there will be no precision in my kicking. The pebble will traverse a certain distance, follow an erratic trajectory, and bounce in unexpected ways. I will have no control of its destiny. I will represent a moving force, but an uncontrollable one. Regardless of the situation, the gutter is not an acceptable destiny. In haste, I kick the pebble to free it from the rubbish. I succeed in changing its surroundings—for the moment.

Perhaps what I need is practice. After a long existence pretending there is an inherent order in life, I need to accept there may be an alternative kind of order. The pebble is certain to demonstrate what that kind of order is about. By kicking it and following it—over and over—I will learn not to expect a linear trajectory. To test my conviction, I aim straight at a lamppost down the street and kick the pebble with a full swing of my leg. And contrary to my prediction, the pebble hits the lamppost in the center of its spine—a perfect direct hit. This unexpected precision is an anomaly; it resides outside of the reigning disorder. That thought reassures me. The pebble and I continue our interlude. The further it lands from me, the stronger its pull, and the faster I run to send it flying again. Together we follow an erratic course through the streets of the village until we arrive at a grand open space.

The sea grows in front of me, unannounced. I can only marvel at its magnificence, its serenity, as it takes over the entire horizon. Behind me, a village and a house that could be mine. In front of me, the rest of this world. This may be what the pebble wanted me to encounter, with its innocent and capricious tumbling. This may be what awaits the traveler with no direction. Or maybe the sea, this immense unknown, has always been here. I understand the pebble, and I must part ways since the material substance surrounding us has changed. We each owe it to ourselves to find our path. So, I kick the pebble one last time with all my force. It ascends over the sea in a soft angle. It grows white wings and flies away into the horizon.

#

Everything changes in front of the sea. I feel reduced, obliterated because I cannot match its might. The only way to eliminate the vast difference between the two of us is for me to integrate with the sea. I could drink all of it and bring it inside of me. But I would grow immense and burst. Conversely, I could let the sea swallow me complete. But I would miss the air. I may need to accept its docile presence and admire it as both a limit and an invitation. The pebble accepted the invitation, most likely for the better. I will consider all possible options, and I will allow the options to consider me as well.

At the edge of the sea, the air takes a few liberties. It swirls around; it prods, it pushes. Maybe it wants to say something to me. I extend my arms and try to grab as much air as possible—nothing much, just a sense of emptiness. But the force of the air is undeniable and needs to be acknowledged. Thus, I face downwind and let the force push me forward. The wind guides my steps along the seashore. At first, I want to run to get ahead of the wind. Running, however, prevents me from truly feeling the wind. In the turbulence, I lose its guiding power. Slowing down my pace and truly sensing the gentle nudge of the wind works better. I welcome the communion between my steps and the wind and move ahead at a facile rhythm.

Once again, I find myself walking along an utterly familiar seashore. Either, I have walked down numerous seashores before, or I have graced the very sand under my feet at another time. Perhaps the image of myself walking down the seashore already existed in my mind, and it is now that it finally becomes a reality. Although, I find it improbable to have had this wonderful experience before and not remember it vividly. What matters is the experience this moment offers, and the freedom it represents. I thus turn the thought process down and proceed with my walk.

I walk in the solitude of the sand. My mind softens in the absence of formed memories. These are the vagaries of time, of purpose—the wind pounds on my back. Beyond the sea, beyond the horizon, beyond the time ahead of me, there is a probable place, a probable self. That is bound to be a long voyage full of familiar unknowns and anxious birds. I do not know if I want to travel that far when what matters seems to unravel under my very feet. This solitude does not harm me; it opens up all possibilities. Above all, the possibility of being traversed by the multiple versions of myself. There is no fear in the transparency of the wind like there is no fear in the transparency of who I am.

The seashore is not eternal. It will extend itself ahead of me until a formidable variation in the terrain will impede my walk: a promontory, a rock formation, the tidal mouth of a river. I will then have to upset my free-flowing walk and face the wind. And in so doing, I will have to make a hard decision and lead my walk willingly—an imposition that will be. So different from the fluid nature of my current walk. If I were to do nothing, that harsh reality is likely to materialize. I can change the course of my walk at any minute and prevent that horrible situation. And that is exactly what I do. I stop abruptly, turn my back to the sea, and start walking inland.

This is also a hard decision, but I turned at a completely unforeseeable point. As a consequence, I find myself without the pushing force of the wind and with no clear idea of my location. The elements around me are familiar in themselves. A tree is a tree, and a house is a house. But the assemblage of them does not produce the fabric of a familiar neighborhood. I could not say that I am lost, for I did not feel properly found before. So, it is possible for this place and situation to be unprecedented. Entering an unknown is the ultimate freedom. We do not need a memory of previous experiences to guide our actions, for what we will encounter is bound to surprise us. Like when we see a face we have never seen before. We cannot love or hate it; we do not owe anything to it. It simply is. In its simplicity, this moment is extremely rich. I wish for all moments to be like this, so open and so encompassing at the same time. And my steps bring me forward with no predetermined direction, and I flow into spaces unknown to me.

I cross many people that seem happy to ignore me. The lack of recognition does not diminish me; to the contrary, I feel rather ample. I wonder if many people knew my face before the crossing. Was I greeted often? Was I identified? Would there be people who miss me on that other side of the street? Those questions imply that this is a different place and a different time. I am not sure that such is the case. So, I continue to walk and accept all the faces that pass by as new faces in this reality. After a while, I decide to sit on a bench and rest. I listen for the ringing of bells to tell me the time. I hear nothing but the sibilance of the wind. Not knowing the time of the day grants me a larger freedom. Yes, I can rest on this bench and let the world be as it pleases.

The world, then, wishes to invite a woman to sit next to me on the bench. She does not ask for permission, nor does she say a single word. She just sits down and looks at me attentively, as if she were studying every angle of my face. I cannot tell what she sees on my face, but she seems rather intrigued. The least I could do is to remain still and let her continue with her analysis. With no apparent rush, she alternates between looking at my face and looking out to the world in front of us. Other than concentrated curiosity, I cannot identify any other emotion on her own face. A face that resembles someone I may have met at some other point in my life, but that now I fail to recognize.

For an instant, I consider greeting her. However, I refrain from starting a conversation because that would interfere with her scrutiny. She must have a reason for doing what she is doing, and I will not derail that process. Why spook the moon at midnight? Better for her to determine the appropriate time to interact with me, assuming, of course, that she wants to interact with me beyond the detailed inspection of my face. The vector of her actions is completely independent from mine. On this bench, we coincide in time and space. But that does not imply the need for interaction. She could easily continue on her way to fulfill what the world has wished for her.

But her face is certainly familiar. She could be a shooting star, burning dust traveling through the atmosphere of my past. She could be the symbol of an old desire I have now forgotten. She could be nothing other than what she is, and my apparent recognition, a mere illusion. There are many people whose faces I have forgotten. And there are many people whose faces I have yet to encounter for the first time. Perhaps we falsely identify similarities in new circumstances as a way to transition from the known to the unknown, like I find this neighborhood somewhat familiar because it may be entirely new and unknown to me, thus frightening. Or I get the impression that the house in which I now live is my house when perhaps I have never entered the place before. Even this life that I am living now is suspect. I may need to believe it is mine because the alternative would be devastating. Regardless of how I explain her apparent familiarity, it is real to me.

The human gaze is a vessel sailing around the world, and I wish to travel along with hers. From my face to the world, from the world to my face, her gaze sails. But she does not invite me to join her; she keeps on sailing alone. I can call out to her like a siren, but why wish on her such a wreckage? I concentrate on the sibilance of the wind, on the fractals of the clouds, on the lazy afternoon light. And realizing that she came to sit on this bench for reasons I will never understand, I watch as she leaves me sitting on the bench and returns to the world and its wishes.

#

Without a pebble to kick around, I need to figure out how to return to the house on my own. A return implies belonging. If I never belonged, then I cannot construe a return. So, I am not returning. Instead, I am heading to the house. That suggests I could never go back to the life I had before the crossing. Probably because the sense of belonging is conspicuously absent. When I turn the scant pages of my memory, belonging is nowhere to be found. Not even during my childhood days do I find roots under my feet. Those were thin days. Furthermore, I have already abandoned my broken toys.

Ahead I march, expecting to arrive at the house at some point. An expectation that grows out of the realm of probability and not of fate. Probability is inherently flawed, whereas fate is inherently oppressive. I prefer a flawed world with its exuberant inconstancy. And I am suddenly regaled when the sound of a wooden flute pierces the crisp of the air. At first, it seems to come from no specific direction. But when I stop my march and concentrate, I get the impression it emanates from a narrow path that gets lost among the houses. I take the path and follow the sound of the flute. The melody is simple but deeply soulful, like a lament, or a cavernous yearning. It lingers in the air like a scent, and I follow it.

With care not to disturb the ephemeral, I take feathery steps toward the music. Lured by its magic, not knowing where I am going, I advance and listen. The path turns in various ways, promising nothing. It meanders among backyards and houses where no one seems to mind about the music. Am I the only person that hears the flute? I come to a stop and pay close attention to the pitch of the flute. But as soon as I stop moving, the melody seems to die away. Where has the melody gone? Has it abandoned me? I wait for a few minutes hoping to hear it again. I hear nothing, only the silence of the world. But as soon as I start walking once more, the melody returns as soulful as before. If the melody returns to me, does it mean that it belongs to me? Or is it me who is returning to the melody?

Nothing seems familiar along this path. In their muteness, the houses and the trees resemble ghosts I have never met. But the melody is as real as the wind and the scent of the far-away sea. So, I stay close to this reality and continue marching toward an improbable belonging. The melodic line and the sound of my steps begin to twist around each other creating a duet of origin and ending. After several intimate cadences, the melody leads me to the house that could be my house. And once I stand in front of this house, I hear not the flute nor my steps, but the melody of being.

Traversing the gate of the house feels natural. I must have entered this house numerous times. There is no rejection here; a tacit embrace is what welcomes me. In principle, any house that opens its doors to me could make me feel welcome. Perhaps it is my expectation that craves the welcoming feeling when stepping into this house. However, I seriously doubt that the house is the only source of such emotion. If the house and I have a history together, I would understand feeling welcome at home. But I am certain that I arrived at this house for the first time only after the crossing. Or so it seems to me. The sense of welcome, however, is undeniable.

I now realize that up until this moment, I have not questioned the fact that I seem to be alone. A few people seem to know me by sight, but other than Babylos, I have not seen anyone whose identity I recognize. Does that make me a detached person? I am not sure because I could come across someone I know at any time. That could happen in the next ten seconds or in the next ten years. Also, there could be other people living in this house that I have yet to encounter. Would that explain the welcoming feeling? I may be completely alone—a strange concept since I have no memory of such an existence—yet, I do not feel lonely.

This house has many rooms, and so does my mind. This house could harbor my own self and other selves. My mind could also contain several versions of who I am. I must enter all the rooms in this house and explore who inhabits them. Even if the rooms are empty, the sentiments of those who lived in them will still be there—an intense experience that will be. What if I come across people or sentiments I abhor? That is the same risk we face when rummaging through the rooms of our mind.

I start at the salon, a large and open space that contains objects of no particular interest except for a few paintings I could admire. Abstract paintings that reveal exactly that which we want to reveal about ourselves.

But I have no inclination for that exercise; I am in search of people and sentiments. Other than I, nobody seems to be in the salon at this time. I can sense joy in this room, as well as fear and hope. But I also sense a mystifying emotion I fail to identify. It does not open itself to me. I look inside my mind for a similar feeling. I find confusing feelings—they are everywhere—but none like this one. I wonder where it comes from, to whom does it belong. It could possibly be an uncertain feeling, and if that were the case, I am ready to accept it—uncertainty, such a universal feeling.

From the salon, a dimly lit corridor leads me into the core of the house. The first door I try opens into a small empty room. There are no traces of anyone using this room currently: no shoes, no clothes, no personal objects. A tall bookcase stands totally empty. There are a desk and a chair, and nothing else. This is not a room, but an absence. I sit at the desk and contemplate the emptiness around me. I marvel at its purity. This space was conceived as a bedroom, or as a studio, I imagine. It was not meant to be an empty room. Or perhaps it was. Not every room in a house requires a living being. This room could be just that: an empty room. In its emptiness, this is a perfect empty room.

The problem is that I feel an absence as if someone has parted from here not too long ago. A perfect empty room should not exude a sense of absence. But this one does, and that forces me to consider time. Absence implies the passage of time. For how long could an absence remain fresh? For hours, days, forever? There is nobody in this room now, but there could have been someone here before, or there will be someone here in the future. Once I step out of the room, there will certainly be an absence, the absence of my very self. The presence that is missing from this room could be a creation of my own. I could be the one expecting that a person be occupying this room. If I were the originator of the sense of absence, then I should explore the rooms of my mind. There is tremendous risk in that proposition.

I walk away from the empty room and open a different door. I am immediately soothed by a pleasant light filtering through the shutters. A soft calm floods this room. Reclining in a corner, I see a wooden flute very similar to the one I used to play before the crossing and almost identical to the one I already found in this house before. Could this be the flute that I just heard on my way to the house? Who would have played it? I consider lifting the flute and trying to play a simple melody, but I refrain myself. This could be my flute, this could be the shadow of another flute, like this could be my house, like this could be my life unchanged. And if my life has not undergone dramatic changes, I should derive enormous pleasure from playing the flute. The air from inside my lungs would turn into musical notes and join with the air outside of me. My body would connect with the universe by means of the music. But what if I produce no sound at all, or if the music refuses to deliver me to the larger universe? I fear the presence of chance inside the calmness of this room. Or perhaps it is not chance per se that I fear, but the negative possibilities dwelling in chance. The positive side of chance, however, would allow me to play the flute like a cherub and be one with the universe.

I refuse to be split by the sword of reductionism. Good versus evil, light versus darkness, beauty versus ugliness, right versus wrong, before versus after the crossing, even death versus life. Why should my world be so small? Why make unnecessary judgments? I could simply allow for all possibilities to align themselves in whatever order suits them. Tossing away any preconceived pressure or dichotomous expectation, I pick up the flute. At first, I consider playing a well-rehearsed melody, something I am supposed to know by heart. But if I were to play an easy piece, I would be yielding to the expectation of having to play well. Playing badly is just as real, and maybe even closer to my condition as a flute player. I take a deep breath and blow into the body of the flute. I launch myself into the fluid and risky world of musical improvisation with no other purpose than the immediacy of playing the music. I allow myself to explore the desire for that which has not yet and may indeed never arrive. In listening to what I am playing, I feel beyond completeness—an abstract embrace of nothing, an arousal of unintended duration.

There is no proof of anything in my playing. Music exists, but not as a result of my playing. The cause of music's existence is just in existence itself. Perhaps it sprouted on this earth without any why or how. Or perhaps it is the sound of our innermost thoughts that we hear, and we call it music. Eventually, the notes become entangled with the light filtering through the shutters and dissipate softly. I recline the flute in the same corner where I found it. I shall let it rest on its own, harboring the potential for unleashing a certain part of me. I can remain in this room for a very long time, but the rest of this house is calling me.

At the end of the corridor, a pair of French doors open into an inner patio where a few potted plants are taking the air. There is a colorful collection of bright flowers that remind me of a time when nothing mattered. I do not recall when or where I felt such freedom, but these flowers elicit such an imprecise memory. I could try to go deep into my mental archives and unearth further details. But what would the purpose be? I could be remembering something that I wished for, but never attained. This may be the embodiment of a forgotten hope. The real question is whether I feel free this very instant. I think I do, and that is what matters. So, I walk around the patio greeting and smelling the flowers and enjoying the freshness of the air. I do not sense an absence in this patio. Perhaps because it is open to the sky, or perhaps because freedom overrides the sense of absence.

If this has always been my house, I would have spent endless hours in this peaceful patio. I could envision myself abandoning all preoccupations and drinking the freedom directly from the air. This place cannot create freedom on its own. It is the convergence of my expectations and the physical characteristics of the patio that ignites a sense of freedom. I imagine that sense of freedom has always emerged upon my entering the patio. Once again, what I recognize is not the actual place but the emotions that such place elicits in my mind. A room or any other place where nothing of emotional importance ever happened would be easily lost from my memory and remain unrecognizable.

I recognized the sea, and I barely recognized the woman that came to sit next to me at the bench. Both must have stirred an emotion in my mind at some point. In this new reality, however, the emotions could be different from what they have been before the crossing. The problem is that this time, the one I am experiencing right now, may not be happening after the crossing. The arrow of time could be broken. Maybe those recognitions are all happening at once on both sides of that horrible wound of a street. But since I am not capable of confirming any of those hypotheses, I need to react emotionally to what I encounter in front of me.

This house contains everything that I may now recognize. It also contains absences. It seems to welcome my presence because no force has kept me from meandering at will. This house is here right now, and I assume it will continue to be. Whatever is known or unknown about this house is not bound to change. I will be the one changing as the encounters accumulate. Consequently, my vision of this house will evolve and become different from the current one. And there is no way of predicting what those changes will be. Given the realization of the impossibility of this moment, I sit in this patio and look up to the sky. I let the sense of freedom traverse my body, my mind. Whatever needs to happen, will happen. Who am I to interfere with the flow of the universe? I exist in this time and perhaps in many other times. I am not afraid.

#

The only thing that I fear is the wound. That street so divisive, so formidable in its brutal capacity to alter my life. I could blame it for having changed the perceived natural order of things. Or maybe it did not change anything—it only revealed. Unlike the sea, a frontier that invites, that street feels like a hard edge, an unbreachable boundary. If I am to exist in this reality, I must do so without fear. The wound, then, makes that impossible. How could I venture out of this house and feel free if I must avoid the hard edge of that street? A street whose name I do not even know. My necessary encounters would be biased. It would be like ignoring the dark side of the moon. There is life on the other side of that street, part of it my own.

I could pretend the street does not exist. A contrived existence that would be for my mind will never accept such deception. The lie will feel like a heavy load on my shoulders when I step out of this house to walk. I have crossed that street, and there is no denying that. Conversely, I could try to walk toward the sea and give the street a wide berth. A futile effort, the need to avoid the street out of fear would make it even more dangerous, menacing. At some point, I will need to confront that street. I will need to confront my fear.

However, the memory of having crossed the street does not make the street real. I could have had a sensation of crossing a street when, indeed, something completely different happened. The street could only be a metaphor for whatever it was that altered the natural order of things. Maybe there was an earthquake, or perhaps a war, or maybe a butterfly fluttered its wings. I see it as a wound, so perhaps it is a deep-seated pain. If the street does not exist as such, there probably was no crossing either. This reality, which I believe is a new one, may be nothing but an old reality in disguise. It is also possible that doubting the existence of the street allows me to control my fear or avoid an unbearable pain.

The freedom I yearn for will only materialize if there is no fear. Fear is a hindrance, a horrible way to lose my humanity. Fear can dismantle my integrity and turn me into slime. Fear will inevitably direct my actions and limit the possibilities of chance. I cannot let fear take hold of my mind. It needs to be confronted, dominated. Because I fear the wound, I need to search for the wound. Even if a determined search for the wound foists an ordered action, I need to begin searching for it. I need to get out of this house and try to find that street again. I am, this moment, totally alone, in order, calm, in the midst of a universal revolution.

I begin by ignoring the rest of the rooms in this house. They could harbor a legion of emotions and elicit a tumultuous river of thoughts. I ignore them not out of fear, for I do not shy away from thinking and feeling, but because the wound will require all my resources. I leave the magnificent patio and make my way to the door of the house. Here I observe the number "3" with reverence. This is the most important coordinate to remember. No shift in reality will dislodge this number from this house. It is an elemental condition; the number will remain unchanged. I continue down the path and through the gate. I am now outside of the house with a single commitment in mind.

What presents the first challenge is the feeble nature of determination. I know exactly what I want to accomplish, and my desire and courage are perfectly aligned. But trying to direct a path into an uncertain future is a questionable strategy. I know I can set my purpose in motion like I can roll a rock down the mountain. The rock will bounce against other rocks and trees and follow an erratic path before finally landing in some unpredictable place. Likewise, my purpose will suffer all the blows life decides to bestow upon it and perhaps be accomplished, or perhaps not. This is not discouraging; the opposite is true. I know what I want, and I will strive for it. Life will intersect me—that is the adventure.

Not knowing exactly which direction to walk is already a good beginning. The only certitude I have is that the street I crossed is under the same sky that is above me right now. I look up and marvel at the immensity of the sky—a shoreless sea, but deeper. I figure that my steps could be informed by the shapes of the clouds. Not the round clouds, for they are immersed in their own gaseous selves, but the elongated and pointy ones. I could follow the direction of the pointy goatees up in the sky. The first cloud to show its face has a particularly long goatee that points south. At once, I start walking in that direction. As in my previous walks, everything seems familiar, but at the same time, unrecognizable. That confirms that my reality has not changed since I last stepped out of the house. I allow for the walk to unravel itself while sustaining a steady pace. After a while, I look up to the sky again but cannot find the original cloud pointing south. It must have vanished, or perhaps it morphed into another cloud. I find another pointy one that leads me west this time. A new direction, a new unrecognizable familiarity. The next time I look up, a magnificent cloud catches my attention. Tinged by a gleam of crimson, it flaunts a prominent and very long goatee. Its force pulls me along, and I accelerate my pace. Houses, trees, lampposts, and dogs pass by me in haste. On the sidewalk, my shadow follows me, oblique, and tells me I am running too fast.

There is no point in rushing; the universe can wait. So, I slow down my pace and assume a more natural rhythm. In spite of the erratic directions suggested by the clouds, I get a sense that the street is near. I can feel it like one feels the night falling—an accumulation of minute changes in light, wind speed, and temperature. Likewise, my needs have changed in small but meaningful ways, from a need to search to a need to encounter. This is happening to both of us, the street, and myself. I may be approaching the street, but perhaps it is the street that is coming to greet me. I will not accept the inevitability of an encounter, for nothing can oblige anything else, but I will certainly embrace the encounter if it were to happen.

Then a cloud suggests I make a sharp turn left and follow a narrow alley. I do as the cloud indicates, and within a few meters, the alley opens up. Right in front of me, the very street I once crossed enters my reality. I recognize the long wound. In its depth, there is an emptiness that escapes naming. At the edge of the wound, I stand, keeping my balance, trying to save myself from falling inside the abyss. I could lose myself inside the monstrous space. That would probably be the end of all potential realities I have yet to understand. But the clouds led me here so I could stand in front of my fear and dominate it. I cannot turn my back now.

Certainly, I came from the other side of the street. Yes, I managed to cross the street and retain an entire sense of myself. That means I did not fall inside the wound. I must have vaulted over the wound somehow. But I know that is not how it happened. A man held my elbow and helped me cross the street. Or did I do it alone? He saw me facing the street with my eyes closed. Then he alerted me about the danger of crossing the street without looking. I understood his concern and accepted his help. He must have been worried about me or perplexed by my actions. I did not expect his presence, nor did I think I needed him. But he delivered me into this reality by helping me across this frontier. I doubt I will ever find that man again.

The long wound is in front of me, but the devilish thing does not react to my presence. Not because I lack a presence, but because the wound itself may be an artifice, a figment of my imagination. No, the wound is real. I respect the wound as I respect the intangible flight of a bird. It is as real to me as the sound of the flute—and that is what matters now. From where I stand, I cannot make out any details of the other side. I believe that somewhere on that side, my previous life somehow lingers. The life that contained me before the uncertainty that now surrounds me. Somewhere there exists a man whose eyes are cascading. And perhaps there is the sound of the flute. Many reassurances are certain to be found on the other side. The problem is that I am afraid of crossing back to where I came from—a fear that binds my feet to the ground.

But I know that I exist otherwise, that a shift in my temporal awareness is only transitory, that beyond the expected is the unknown. I accept the improbable and welcome alternating layers of causality and chaos. I accept the color purple knowing that it is sometimes blue or red. And accepting all possibilities, I unbound my feet and my mind. I venture away from the wound, back into this new unknown and toward the house that could be my house.

#

This feels like an old afternoon. It has been around for a few hours only, but it weighs as if ancient. The heat must be culpable, or perhaps the accumulation of discarded thoughts. Yes, I have done a lot of thinking this afternoon. I have also lived a lot this afternoon. Outside my window, the world seems oblivious to my concerns. It is as if we exist in different planes. The world, and everything within it, revolves around my mind without touching me. There are times when I feel as if I were an integral part of that world, as if we shared a common destiny. That does not happen too often.

I contemplate people walking past my window and doubt they know where they are going. They may think they know, and once they arrive somewhere, they convince themselves that they intended to be there. Reality is much less organized than that. People move as loose vectors and are impacted by erratic forces. With each impact, the course of the vector changes and reality is reset over and over. If that were common knowledge, the world would lose its orderly mask, and people would probably be terrified. I am not terrified, but I do not expect an orderly life either.

I wonder what awaits me this afternoon. Out there, in the open world, there may be someone or something expecting to cross my path. That means I would have to live even more than I have already lived this afternoon. Maybe that is what makes this afternoon feel so old and heavy. The expectations may be dragging me down. However, I do not have to accept any such inevitability. I could discard the concept of expectancy and enjoy the rest of the afternoon free as a bird. I could do as I wish, for I have no master. At least, I think I have none.

Not feeling completely attached to this house allows me to leave it behind with ease. The house has nowhere to go. The house also knows I have nowhere to go. We understand each other. We have no regrets. So, I step out the door and enter this world that cares little for me. Not because the world does not want to care, but because it is not in its nature. If I said that I do not care for the world, I would be lying. I care tremendously for every plane of reality that intersects my life. I just do not know what to expect when I step outside of this house.

This afternoon, the first element to embrace me is the free-flowing air. I am happy with the encounter. It soothes me. It carries a few recognizable scents, jasmine, for example. I think of the little white flowers and how they line the path leading to the sea. I cannot smell the sea from where I am, but I know it is alive somewhere. The air also carries a faint conversation happening somewhere in the distance. The words are not intended for me, so I let them fly away. The next thing I encounter is people's faces. We react to a face as we react to a flag or a sign on the road. We anticipate something when we come across a face. But a face may not be the visual representation of the being behind the face. In this world, faces are not inclined to symbolize the minds they usher in. Sometimes, with a powerful, enigmatic capacity, a face can unleash an entire life story, with its past, suffering, and fears. Only sometimes.

The first face I come across is that of my apparent neighbor, whose eyes seem to be cascading. He avoids facing me. I think he fears I will ask him questions about his health or the weather. None of which is of interest to me. But I would like to know more about his understanding of this world and how his life fits in it. Maybe he anticipates I will ask those very questions. That would certainly cause his eyes to cascade. But the truth is that I have never said anything to him other than a casual greeting. So, perhaps I am the one avoiding him and not the other way around. He does look down as he passes by.

Further down the street, I stumble upon a woman sitting on the curb all by herself. There is a certain emptiness around her. I could change my direction and avoid her completely, but that is not what I do. She watches me as I approach her. When I sit next to her on the curb, I am confronted with an inexpressive, therefore frightening face. It seems as if her soul has abandoned her. My instinct is to leave at once, but I do not move. She does not move either; she looks at me from the vacancy of her face. I wait for her to start speaking, but she does not say a word. The air stops its free flow. The world comes to a total arrest.

I wonder who this woman is and by what incantation she has materialized in my life. I have never seen her before, in this improbable neighborhood, or anywhere else. She may be the princess of a faraway land, or a slave, or perhaps a survivor from a useless war. She could be any of that or nothing at all. The truth is that I was the one approaching her. I altered my immediate reality to include sitting next to her. However, she could have been sitting at the curb, expecting my inevitable arrival. That would imply she had prior knowledge about me, and that is an impossibility.

Since the world has stopped turning, I have no urgency in trying to resolve the genesis of this encounter. Time has no essence now. Thus, I unambiguously observe her as she observes me. A survey of her features makes me feel unsettled. Her eyes do not plead, nor do they marvel. Her lips rest empty of words. The muscles of her jaw show no tension. The sum of all her features impedes an expression from forming on her face. She could not be read, nor understood, by the simple scrutiny of her face. No change in her face reveals what might be stirring within her.

Could I get to know a person like this woman? Maybe, but she would need to communicate all her feelings by means of her voice. Her words, then, would become her face. But, would there be a point in looking at her face if it shows no emotion? Probably, since we are accustomed to doing so. We even look at the eyes of a person wearing a mask. Perhaps we place too much emphasis on people's faces, faces that come to be as the result of incidental genetic liaisons and unforeseeable tears. What appears to be an emptiness behind the face of this woman may be completely the opposite. She may be fathoms deep. The problem, however, is that she has not spoken a single word. Her silence denies me her face. I could ask questions and try to look inside her. The danger is that she may start talking and unleash unknown butterflies. Indeed, I am afraid of what she would say.

In my core, I have the strange impression that we

belong to the same species, this woman and me. I can imagine her pondering the meaning of my face. She is certain to find my expression intriguing, if not revelatory. Most likely, she will not believe what she sees on my face. If she were to believe, her own face would turn into a dark pond. She may be wondering why I sat down next to her. She may be waiting for me to start talking.

I decide to accept this moment for what it is: a miracle of the unstable circle of fate. And as such, I will not raise any conjecture as to the purpose of the encounter, nor will I look for its meaning. Then I stand up next to this woman and regard her face a little longer. With a calm and deliberate gesture, I grab her by the elbow and help her get on her feet. We stand next to each other as two trees that have grown together. The wind makes her leaves flutter, and I accept those as her words. There is nothing to fear. I start walking back to the house while still holding onto her elbow. She comes along, her face still an enigma, but with clear and unyielding steps. She must be a natural wanderer, for she offers no resistance or hesitation. Either we have walked like this before, or we will walk like this from now on.

When we reach the house, she does not hesitate before opening the gate and letting herself inside the short path leading to the porch. She then waits for me at the door. If I hope to understand in order to accept things, the circle of fate would strangle me. Thinking beyond the immediacy of the moment will keep me from surrendering. Incomprehension is not the opposite of comprehension, only a corollary. I need to surrender now. And the only way to do it is by opening the door and letting her enter the heart of this house.

Once inside the house, she moves with ease. She must be smelling the fragrances, listening to old whispers, even feeling the absences. I follow her without interfering with her exploration. She traverses the corridors like the wind. She enters the rooms; she opens the windows. She then goes to the kitchen and pours two glasses of my favorite red wine. This is clearly not foreign territory to her; she has a memory of this house. I have no recollection of her presence in this house, but that does not mean she has been absent. This may be her house as much as it may be mine. This time she grabs my elbow and leads me through the French doors into the patio. The sky comes to greet us, and so does the freshness in the air. I wonder if this patio ignites a sense of freedom inside of her.

She drinks from her glass, a gesture as ancient as it is beautiful. She then repeats the gesture. In an attempt to join her purpose, I drink from my glass as well. I wait a few minutes while regarding the expression on her face. However, the effect the wine has on her remains a mystery for her expression stays the same—a tabula rasa. Nothing on her face reflects the inexplicable changes in her immediate reality. But, perhaps nothing has changed at all for her. She could be doing what she has always done on a day like today. I have the impression that I found her sitting at the curb, that I approached her and led her back to this house. An impression that only exists within the realm of my perceived reality. Alternatively, she could have been waiting for me at the curb in order to return back to her house in my company. The mechanics of the two events appear to be the same, but the underlying purposes bringing them about differ tremendously.

The world is about to tremble within me. I hold my wine glass steady and hope for the winds to soften the blow. Nothing shakes, nothing quivers. I must be assimilating this new unknown. Her presence may be taking root in this patio. I am prepared to accept this actuality as long as my own presence is not denied. This may still be my house, and perhaps I even live here. And on this patio, I drink my wine and my freedom. As I have these thoughts, I wonder why the need to assert anything. We cannot assert a purpose, nor can we assert any outcomes. Perhaps we can assert a truth, although in a relative world, truth is polyvalent. The best would be for me to remain calm and alert at the same time.

Realizing she has almost finished her glass of wine, I go to the kitchen to fetch the bottle. Upon my return to the patio, I find the woman moving from one potted plant to another, sampling the various scents the flowers can offer. She pauses in front of each flower as if becoming acquainted with the fragrance or with a memory.

She inhales the intimate depth of a rose deeply. She then confronts an irritated carnation. She then seeks the perfume of an introverted violet. And the procession continues until she has taken inside herself a little of every flower. The ease of her movements tells me that freedom is with her as well. When she sees me holding the bottle of wine, she extends her arm, indicating she would like some more. But not a word she speaks, nor her face registers any expression.

The woman then makes her way to the very center of the patio. She stands there as if she were in absolute control of her kingdom. An unwavering and majestic image this is. As I observe her, I wonder if I have seen this image before, if I have ever encountered a silence so formidable and profound. And at the very instant that I ponder the concept of silence, she begins to hum a soft and mysterious melody—notes of inherent simplicity and inexplicable somberness. I recognize the structure of the melodic phrases. She seems to be singing in an ancient Phrygian mode, the third mode. And I am impressed by the way she modulates her voice with understated grace while not articulating a single word. The enchanting melody emanates from the very center of this woman's self. These must be the feelings that her face is absconding.

The air is free to come into this patio and touch both of us. The woman is free to sing her innermost feelings and retain her barren face. The flowers are free to exude their essence without restraint. I am free to integrate this moment into my reality. The world is free to contain us all. The cause of our existence is just in existence itself.

Part Two:

WHITE CLOUDS

Why not play the flute? The wooden instrument leans against the wall in anticipation. What aspects of my life rely upon me playing the flute? If the flute became mute for some reason, would I still be a flute player? I do not define myself as a flute player, but other people may just do that. I do not think of the flute as a flute, like I do not think of this house as a house. The function cannot exhaust the vast possibilities of an object or a person. The flute is still a flute even when I am not playing it. But it is also the relic of an ancient New Zealand kauri tree forty-thousand-years-old. It has a nobility that extends beyond its capacity to generate beautiful sounds. The flute and I are not different—we cannot be contained.

I lift the flute and begin to play a low, deep melody. An improvised basso continuo to sustain my thought process. The melody ascends and fills the room; it reverberates slowly. This is not the sound the audience normally hears in a concert hall. This is a neural sound vibrating at 432 hertz like the rest of nature. The wooden fibers in the flute, the air, and all the cellular mass comprising my body vibrate in unison. Unencumbered, I am free to explore the intrinsic regularities and irregularities of this life of mine.

When I try to remember how I became what I now consider to be myself, I realize that I am missing memories. The movie of my life does not playback in a continuous fashion. There are large sections where the screen only shows a gray snow. Those could be trivial moments not worth remembering. Or those could be horrifying moments now repressed by a protective mind. Regardless of their emotional impact, those moments could have an important role in the ultimate trajectory of my life. Assuming, of course, that there is only one trajectory. Perhaps I see those moments as gray snow because they do not pertain to the reality at hand, the one available to me. I can imagine a complete negative of the film where what is now visible becomes gray snow, and what is hidden from me becomes a clear and vivid image. The problem is that I am not in charge of the projector.

Those are the challenges when dealing with the past. We attribute a large importance to what already happened when we barely know what really happened. Even if we knew how things took place, we would probably interpret those events from the standpoint of our current frame of mind. We would be painting our past life with today's colors. And even more dangerous, we would link one event after another, creating a retrospective linear association that would seem logical to us, when in reality, events unfolded by accident. There is a great risk in looking back.

I continue playing the flute but change the melody to a more complex one. Focusing on what I am playing will distract my mind. I can trick myself into forgetting that I cannot remember the past. The first impulse is to play an intricate composition requiring my complete attention. But why would I do that? The best would be to let the notes play themselves. In this improvisatory mode, I blow air into the flute and let my fingers dance as they will. This must be the sound of chance. Even if I play a progression within a scale, the alternating variations occur on their own. I know there are more notes in the universe than the ones I can play. But in spite of the limited range of playable notes available to this flute, they manage to interact with each other in a myriad of ways. With each breath, a musical passage is born out of the flute. Each passage contains its own individual structure where notes owe their existence to the previous notes. And with each of my breaths, a new chain of notes ensues. After their relatively short lives, most passages end on the tonal note. But each of them follows a divergent path.

The flute becomes quiet. All the echoes and reverberations have exhausted their lives. There is silence again. I listen for any other music, but no sound reaches my ears. There are no human sounds, either. I could think out loud and hear myself talking, but that would be redundant; my thoughts are already loud enough. Taking advantage of this quiet moment, I reflect on the presence of the woman whose face denies me any answers. She used her voice to convey something I could not understand. Was she telling a full story or was she merely improvising? Like myself, she could have allowed for the sound of her voice to oscillate at will. And she sang in such an ancient Phrygian mode, so cyclical and enchanting. I wonder if her voice originated from one emotional theme or multiple ones. I also wonder why she decided to share her voice with me. When I play my flute in public, I hide my emotions; I am only performing. But when I infuse my personal silence with the sound of the flute, I am in touch with the white center of me.

She sang for me. Perhaps because she is incapable of speaking, her speech may be as absent as her facial expression. She may have already expended all available expressions. Or her expressions are tied up expressing themselves somewhere else. How could someone lack the most essential human capacity, the capacity to let others know how we feel? Her singing matters to her; it must. That is how she fills the silence inside.

Let the flute rest and dream of being a tree. At this moment, I have a need for confirmation. By questioning the meaning of her singing, I imply there is a fundamental order to her actions. It occurs to me that we may not need order to live. There may be no pattern to follow and the pattern may not even exist. I could confront this woman and ask her if, indeed, she sings because it is orderly for her to do so. However, trying to elicit an explanation from her reveals my own need for a certain order. I could simply confront her and ask nothing. But my presence in front of her would be understood as a question, or perhaps as an answer.

Through the house, I move in search of the woman. All the spaces in the house seem to respect my need for searching. They remain very quiet as I move through them. How long ago did I see her is a mystery to me. I know I played the flute, but for how long? For how many days? Confirmation of time is not important, so I put aside those concerns. Eventually, I reach the patio where I saw her last. And when I go through the French doors, I am pleased to find her there, still standing in the center of the patio. Like in the rest of the house, there is only silence in the air.

Upon hearing my steps, she turns around to face me. Once more, I regard her inexplicable visage. That which she sees, and does not speak of, frightens me. I realize that her lack of expression may encompass an infinite richness. The absence of emotion impedes an attachment to any particular feeling, positive or negative, and consequently, it allows for the potential of all possible feelings. Like a field covered by fresh snow, where there is not only one shade of white, but all the possible shades of white that exist. The vastness of her feelings must be extraordinary. By not expressing anything, she expresses everything.

Certainly, I could not have met a person like her and forgotten all about it. I would have been impacted in the same way that I am impacted now. Her unusual presence could not have been ignored. My reality, then, would have been dented. However, if she is part of my past, then she is a missing memory. And like her, there may be many more memories that escape me. But if she were only part of my immediate present, then I gladly welcome the chance to experience her existence in this house. Nevertheless, this probability is challenged by the ease with which she handles herself, by her obvious knowledge of my favorite red wine. Those details are imbued with a sense of past. Once again, the problem resides in trying to find an order. If I were confident that there is no order or pattern to follow, I would be free to regard her face without having to question anything. Still, considering all the uncertainties that surround me, I think I should pause and acknowledge the freedom the patio has to offer.

I wait for her to move, but she does not take a step. I wait for her to sing again, but she remains silent. I wait for the wind to flood the patio and change this reality, but instead, a stillness sets in. Nothing outside of me seems to evolve at this moment. With no exterior force hampering me, I am free to act as I wish. This world is looking up to me in expectation. Does that mean that I am the only entity responsible for what will happen next? That is unlikely, for I am not the center of this or any other world. It is completely possible that I am going through all these considerations in a timeless reality. The thoughts I have may not occupy even a second. If time has not elapsed at all, then this woman could not have had the chance to move, nor hum any melody. The wind could not have had the opportunity to stretch out and touch me. Time needs to expand and make enough space for things to happen. Any expectations I may harbor could only be realized if there is enough time to fit them in. Perhaps the freedom I experience in this patio is the result of a timeless reality. Yes, I am free to feel and wish whatever I want. And as long as time does not elapse, everything remains within the realm of possibility. Thus, I should not be disappointed.

I am not disappointed. I welcome the nakedness of this moment, the thin layer of reality that tries to expand itself over the short horizon of this instant. I am happy to accept the possibility of not knowing. If this reality is nothing but an interim period with no weight at all, I am prepared to deal with the consequences. All I have to do is wait and accept whatever the world will present to me. And once I am presented with a reality to consider, I can always ponder and wait. As long as time has not undertaken its brutal rhythm, I have a universe of opportunities to evaluate. I can always hold back my reactions, remain impassive, withhold my intentions. I can always stay outside of time.

I hold my breath to verify if the river of life still traverses me. Sooner or later, the cells in my body will clamor for air. That will be the natural response of the animality that resides within me. If I were not to experience agonizing suffocation, then either I have not held my breath, or I am effectively existing outside of time.

I could also observe what surrounds me for evidence of movement, a physical phenomenon that relies on the passage of time. But the stillness is such that not a single leaf or flower wavers. An angular shadow looks the same as it did when I walked into the patio. As for the woman, she has not made a single gesture since I started regarding her. With no external points or reference, I depend on my need for air to account for the passage of time.

Could it be that the temporal needs of the organic matter that comprises our body and that of our mind are totally different? If thoughts could occupy an infinite span of time, why would they be housed inside our bony skull, bathed in fluids, and gasping for air? The timeless essence of the human condition, the one quality which separates us from all other beasts, finds itself trapped inside mundane, decaying flesh. A design, so mistaken that only a distracted god could have conceived of it. Not only do the thoughts occur in absence of prescribed time, but if they were to be written down, they truly have the possibility of lasting forever.

Then, all at once, I feel a burst from deep inside myself as if molten words were erupting while a great transient wind floods the patio. The colors of all the flowers shatter and the woman sings a wordless sung cleaving the space between sadness and joy. I am not sure why all of this is happening, or even when. This could be the intervention of arbitrary forces in nature. But what I find intriguing is that when I try to look at myself, I cannot find me.

#

The moment I leave the house, the sky comes out to see what my intentions are. Not that the sky has any influence on the occurrences of the day, but as an overseer, it probably feels a certain obligation to know. I wonder how the sky feels when there is a heavy rain or a dense fog. Does it need to see us to know what we are doing, or does the sky know what our thoughts are? From high above, given the immense perspective, the sky must be able to understand and anticipate a particular chain of events. Intentions may be evident when observed from that point of view. That is the reason why most religions set their mighty god up in the sky. As long as there is an overseer who guarantees that the chain of events follows a determined trajectory, we can relax and comfortably forget that accidents are caused by nothing but chance.

The hope that my expectations will be quickly realized falls out of my hands. I was not expecting much when I left the house, but I was clearly not counting on coming face-to-face with Babylos this moment. He looks unwell. He seems rather agitated. From what I can gather, he must be coming from the sea. His clothes are wet, and he is barefoot. I know he likes to go swimming when he feels lonely. Once far away from the shore, he calls out his own name. When nobody responds, he swims back to shore. That seems to calm him down. But he is not in a calm state right now. He starts talking about a stabbing pain on the left side of his chest. He points to his heart. He then says that his left arm does not want to move, that he had a difficult time swimming back to shore. The intensity of his facial expression scares me. I reach out to feel his left arm, but he pulls away from me. When I ask what I could do for him, he responds by shaking his head and saying that he needs no help.

Babylos turns around and starts walking back to the sea. He moves at a steady pace, and I follow him. He knows that I am following him but will not turn back to face me again. Once we reach the shore, he stops abruptly. He remains standing there for a while. It is sunny and clear, so the sky must be watching him as intently as I am. Then his body begins to shake, and he falls to his knees. Two seconds later, he falls forward, and his head comes crashing against the sand. He then rolls over to his side and pleads for me to leave him alone. He is already alone; he has always been alone.

With great effort, he gets back on his feet and turns around to look at me. Through his pain, he regales me with an ample smile. I can see the sand between his teeth. He then walks into the incoming surf and starts to swim away from the shore with a single-arm stroke. He calls out his own name, Babylos, Babylos, Babylos…

A total inversion of the sky. The sea now covers my head, and it stays fixed above me. It does not drip a single drop of water. Below me, then, all of the sky. I did not anticipate this conundrum, and I do not particularly like it. I think of ways to change this situation, but nothing occurs to me. So, I simply float between the two blues and hope not to drift too far. I cannot hear Babylos calling himself any longer. He must have ascended deep into the sea like the admiral he is. I never know with Babylos.

The wind comes to make things intelligible. I feel it blowing hard on my back and pushing me away from the shore as the sky returns to the top of the world. I do as the wind commands, and consequently, I find myself heading in the direction of the concert hall where I believe I play my flute once in a while. Naturally, the wind can shift, and so would my path if I am obedient. In reality, I have no clear reason to head for the concert hall, but maybe the wind knows something I ignore. I agree with the subtle impositions of the wind as it continues to blow in the same direction. The concert hall soon materializes in front of me. I recognize the building, majestic, even venerable, but I doubt the building recognizes me.

I greet the guard whose name I cannot remember, and he returns the gesture. Inside the hall, a silence reigns supreme. There is no concert at this time, and nobody is rehearsing. I try to listen for any loose note floating in the air, but nothing reaches my ear. The concert hall is like an oyster shell with no pearl inside. The wind already sacked the place of all the notes and all the brilliance that it ever possessed. I am certain that I have played my flute within these walls; there is no doubt. But where are those notes now? Do they continue to exist? Do they even sound the same as when I played them? What purpose do they ultimately serve? Yes, the notes may exist, but how do we know they exist in a continuum of time?

I resist the impulse to answer any of those questions. The danger resides in the possibility of not finding an answer, which may result in keeping me from playing another note in my lifetime. Sometimes it is better not to know. The answers we unearth may not be the real ones or may not belong to this time. Nothing, not even the wind, can shed light on those questions. So, I remain quiet and absorb the silence that fills the empty hall. I bring my mind to a complete resting state. But then, slipping through a crack in the silence, I hear a faint voice. At first, I believe it must be just a memory since I am completely alone inside the hall. But the voice gradually grows and becomes a chant that overflows the space inside the hall. I listen attentively even when my instincts tell me not to listen at all. There is no doubt; the chant pertains to the woman who inhabits the house. I recognize the melody; I recognize the Phrygian mode. The melody bounces and twirls, it germinates, it flourishes, it paints the walls. I accept its presence; I take it deep into my consciousness.

The concert hall does not know this woman. It has never hosted her voice. But at this moment, it seems as if she is supreme, as if the world needs to genuflect to her chanting. And the immediacy of this experience makes me wonder if she is more than a face in the patio. She could be integral to my life as a flute player. She could define me in ways I cannot elucidate. Regardless, her chant continues to breathe inside the walls of the hall. First soft, as if nothing mattered, then intense, as if dispensing life. I bend with the emotional pressure. I grab onto myself. Her power is not in the meaning of the chant, for there are no words to elucidate, but in the desperation they elicit. Inside the hall, listening to her voice, I feel like an impostor. She projects a veritable reality while I only doubt if anything is real.

The voice vanishes, but not the presence of the voice. I look at every corner of the hall and find an expected emptiness. Nobody is here at this time. Her voice did not originate from the acoustic capacities of the concert hall. Her voice seems to have materialized out of my need to listen for it. I may have thought about her voice with such intensity as to will her into existence. When called upon, the mind cannot resist.

I find myself exiting the concert hall to avoid any further confusion between what is and what is not. Better to take my chances in the open streets where the wind is free to come and go as it pleases. I attempt to set a course to follow, but I dread making the commitment. Setting a goal would almost guarantee that such goal will not be accomplished. Considering the vagaries that colonize my world, to aim is to miss. Thus, letting go of all constraints, I take a few random steps down a street. When I regard the passers-by, they all seem like strangers to me. That does not mean that I am a stranger to them, since I may have used this street to walk back and forth between the house and the concert hall. Yes, I always carry my flute with me when walking this way. So maybe I am not interacting with the world in the same way as I do when I carry my flute. But the flute cannot define who or what I am, absolutely not. Other people, however, may not associate the person they see this very instant with the one they are used to seeing carrying the flute. This moment I am someone else to them, and reciprocally, they may seem like strangers to me.

Unannounced, a short man stops me to ask for directions. He wants to know how to get to the concert hall. I ask him if he thinks that I am a musician. He says that he is a musician himself but that he could not tell whether I am a musician or not. I do not elaborate any further and tell him that if he continues to walk straight, he will soon reach the concert hall. He continues his march, and I wait a few seconds before turning around to see where he is heading. When I take a long view down the street where I came from, I realize I am not in the street where I thought I was. Clearly, the short man is not going to find the concert hall as I told him. But less clear is how I got to be where I now find myself. I can blame the wind for shifting my course, or the passers-by for distracting me. I can also blame myself for wanting to stay within the constraints of a well-known street, thus assuring that I would wind up elsewhere. I am not lost; I am displaced. Yet another confirmation that the world has a tendency to shift continuously. With every step I take, the world swivels slightly under my feet. I accept the displacement like I accept a shifting wind.

Chaos readies itself again. I can sense it. To avoid the bruises, I let go of everything. I better not hold onto anything at all, especially the reality that jumps in front of me. Like the short man asking for directions. How do I know he really intends to go to the concert hall? How do I know he is a musician as he told me? I will never know the answer to those questions. And that is the problem; reality is nothing but a series of unanswerable questions. Holding onto reality is like holding onto quicksand. Thus, I just march ahead at a comfortable pace, hoping to get somewhere at some point.

There comes a time when what matters is not what awaits me at the end of the road, but the journey that will take me there. A journey that cannot be traced ahead of time. A journey that reveals itself in the very instant in which I engage in the journey. It is the logical result of all the forces that act upon me at any particular time. The sun, the incline of the sidewalk, the memories competing for space, the breeze, the child in his scooter that cuts my way, the drop of sweat running down my cheek, all of them, together, define the journey. I may succeed in trying to ignore a few of these forces with the hope of gaining some control. But like cutting the head of the Hydra, when a force is suppressed, two stronger forces spring forward to take its place.

I remember when, as a child, I thought I could walk over the clouds. They extended themselves far into the horizon, forming an inviting path. A white path I could follow for a long time. I did not fear falling through the clouds. They were solid enough to support my weight. But I never took that journey. Not because I doubted the possibility of the journey, but because the path was too beautiful, too pristine. My steps would have soiled the clouds, changing their whiteness forever. I did not dare to alter such a perfect path. Perhaps clouds are the only solid substance to hold my steps. Everything else is solid only in appearance. Bricks, gravel, or stones cannot hold me. I may walk, and not having any support, fall inside myself where there is a child looking at the clouds.

After a long or a short walk—I cannot really tell—I come to stand in front of what could be my house. I recognize the number "3" on the door. I try to listen for the voice of the woman, but no chant reaches my ears. When I look through the windows, nothing seems to move inside. There is a familiar stillness in the air. However, a sense of apprehension begins to grow inside of me as I cannot anticipate what I will find when I enter the house. Maybe there are clouds inside.

#

Nobody knocks at the door. Nobody presumes to come into this house. This is only natural as I have no rendezvous with anyone today or anytime soon. I do not expect the outside world to come into my world. This situation suits me well, for I need to clarify a few concerns within myself. I sit down and rest calmly while contemplating the most surprising mental imagery. First, a harlequin jumps in front of me, wearing the mask of an old hermit. I have seen his face before. He lives alone and wants no interaction with anybody else other than himself. Years have gone by since he spoke to another person. Not because he dislikes people; to the contrary, he enjoys company. What he dislikes are the lies. He made a pact with himself to eliminate all pretense and simulacra from his interactions with others. The old hermit succeeded in his stratagem, and for that reason, he has not spoken to anyone else since he made up his mind. The mask of the old hermit does not evoke loneliness. In fact, he wears a radiant smile.

The next harlequin to appear wears the mask of a young princess. Her beauty walks ahead of her. Nobody recognizes her agonizing desire to be liked. She is wanted for her flesh, not for what she thinks. She once spoke her heart, and nobody listened because everyone was mesmerized by her beauty. She has stopped speaking, although she entertains complex thoughts while wearing a radiant face.

Another harlequin wears the mask of a harlequin. When he takes his mask off, he finds himself again. And that is the problem. He then puts back on the harlequin mask and pretends that nothing has happened. When I look at him, he looks back at me as if he were looking at his own mask. He does not radiate much, but he seems very real to me.

Then comes a harlequin wearing my face as his mask. I awaited this one, and I fear him tremendously. I dare not talk to him. Let him parade in front of me, displaying his colorful costume while I watch him from the corner of my eye. I doubt I can confront him face-to-face. He knows that I am watching him, and that is why he jumps and makes all sorts of pirouettes, provoking me. As I feared, this harlequin will not go away until I acknowledge his presence and his impact on me. Perhaps he feels the same apprehension when looking at my face from behind the mask of my face. There is no other option, so I prepare to encounter that which is me in the other. Thus, I stand firm on my feet and look straight at my face as a mask. I recognize what I see on my face, most of it. But there are crevices that harbor shadows of a life I do not recollect. I wonder if the unfamiliar expression in my eyes belongs to me. Perhaps there is more to me that has, thus far, escaped me. And I hope that otherness is at least radiant.

To avoid harming any of my potential realities, I close my eyes and usher the harlequins away from my field of vision. I am not dismantling them; I am only clearing my awareness. Because once I feel unfettered, I could continue with my explorations. There must be stories inside this house that predate the current moment and define the way I think about myself. The problem is that the various rooms only speak in whispers making it difficult for me to hear the story of myself. With the exemption of the patio, where marvelous developments have taken place, every other space appears rather reserved. Perhaps this is how we protect ourselves from the unwanted noise of our memories. But regardless of the dangers involved, I move inside this house as if it were mine, as if it held my life in its core.

Through a half-open door, I come inside a room I cannot recognize. Initially, I consider turning around and exiting at once, the air having a musty quality and the light being infirm. But I pause and reflect on the potential for elucidation contained within this room. If my immediate reaction is to flee, there ought to be a counter-reaction just as strong, forcing me to remain in this room and face the unknown. There is nothing to fear. In the end, this could be my house, and any unpleasantness should be known to me already. I stand in the center of the room where the only furniture is a small table on top of which a book lies open. A leather-bound book this is. And that leads me to believe that the book must be important to me or to those who printed it. I notice that the book is open on its first few pages. Either I have read the very beginning of this book and set it on the table for future completion, or its spine cracked at its weakest point, exposing its innards in a random way. I cannot tell.

With hesitation, I take the book in my hands and read from the open page. The words tell the story of a man who learns about his future from a book he finds inside his house. Naturally intrigued, I read a little further. The book goes on to reveal that what the man thought was his future, were indeed events he had already experienced in his own past. But when the man tries to remember those events, all he finds are empty rooms in his memory. The man in the story decides to continue reading, and in the process, he discovers his future as if it had already happened, of which he has no recollection. Thus, his future reads like a big unknown, even if he has already lived through it. I put the book down and refuse to read any further. I can only wonder if this book was written for me a long time ago.

On the way out of the room, I traverse a corridor where the lights are bright enough for me to focus on a strange painting hanging on the wall. I have seen this painting before, but I have never looked at it. Perhaps the strange qualities have pushed me away. It is possible to live in the presence of an object and not know the object. Like it is possible to live in the company of a person and not know the person. The strangeness is manifested in the way the painting represents nothing, an abstraction in the pure sense of the word. But at the same time, now that I look at it with intention, it seems to open inwards and invites me to a private seance. The colors are not well-defined, and without images, what remains is a sensation of looking inside a person's mind. The attraction is not based on the sensorial experience the painting creates, but in the promise that a mind could be found inside the painting. But whose mind could that be? The mind of the painter? The mind the painter wanted to portray? The mind of the viewer?

If the mind of the painter or a surrogate is the one depicted in the painting, then the image would have been fixed and determined from the very conception of the work. But if the painting is meant to reflect the mind of the viewer, then it is destined to be eternal, changing over and over with the gaze of each passer-by, never remaining the same painting. I take the risk to look deep into the painting. Unlike a mirror that would return an intact and accurate visual image of myself, what I first see inside the painting is a nebulous space, vast and imprecise. I cannot find me. I sense I am somewhere in there, but I cannot find me. I stand firm while continuing to pierce the insides of the painting. Some of me will have to emerge. Then, gradually, a few clouds begin to take shape. White clouds, they are unpolluted. They do not fill the vastness of the space; they only line the visible contours. Then I see the fuselage of fast-moving objects, or people, traversing the unending space. If they belong to a specific time, then time is fleeting. Darkness infiltrates and dominates the entire space, the longest night, or doubts, or that which I do not want to think about. A pale light dares to push away some of the darkness and installs itself with pride. Then the smell of burnt sugar and faded jasmine, unseen but very present. And when I think I am about to recognize a place or a person, the space opens up even further and draws me deeper inside. This is my vastness, an unrecognizable space.

I remain in the quiet vastness, aware and calm, looking, expecting nothing. But nothing is not what the painting delivers, for a figure begins to emerge as if being born out of the light, out of the entrails of the painting. This figure could be an animal, maybe a lost memory, or perhaps the embodiment of my own hope. I try to visualize its contours, but the edges vanish away into the vastness. I know I must wait and allow for the small miracles to materialize. And I do so. Gradually, then, the figure of a woman begins to take shape in the upper right corner of the painting. Not an entire woman, only the semblance of a face. The image coalesces into itself; it seems to boil on immaterial substrate, it evolves without formally evolving. It seems as if the face wants to reveal itself, but then it falls within itself revealing nothing. I know that if I am patient, the painting will speak its colors.

If this is my personal vastness, no other being could be found inside of me. I may project an otherness, but an otherness within the boundaries of myself. A woman could exist inside this painting only as an external reflection. These thoughts trouble me, and as a result, I collect myself; I draw my wings close to my body and continue to regard the depths of the painting. In the supreme silence of this moment, I hear nothing, but unannounced, the sense of a presence slips into my awareness. Immersed as I am into the space of the painting, the only presence to be felt must come from the outside. I deepen my quietness and turn to my ears and skin for sensorial clues. But I feel nothing and hear nothing. The only thing that changes is the image of the woman in the painting. It becomes more real yet unrecognizable. Slowly, her face begins to integrate eyes, nose, even lips. The boundaries of her face become tangible, instilling in her a corporeal reality. And the more real she becomes, the more her face attains the defining shadows that tell a person's history. Once the features of the face come into a perfect focus, at once, I realize the absence of expression. Could she be inside my world? The same woman that inhabits my patio and knows the wine I drink. Is she no other than me?

My ears, then, capture the first notes of the same chant that endeared me before. The Phrygian inspired melody begins to flood the corridor where I stand observing this painting, regarding my vastness, confronting once more this enigmatic face. And like the Pantheon in the morning, the sense of a presence weighs on me. I hold my breath and listen. As I welcome the otherness, the surprising presence becomes preeminent just behind my back. I capitulate to that which asks to intersect my reality. I turn around to confront the source of the melody. And as I expected and feared, the woman whose face has yet to deliver a meaningful expression stands behind me looking straight into the painting, her image reflected above my right shoulder. She continues to sing, and in so doing, she invades my world. She forces me to consider what to accept as mine, how to understand my reflected world. If the painting returns the image of what stands in front of it, has she now become more intimately intertwined with me? Do I have a choice in what I am becoming?

Most often, I expect the unexpected. But when simultaneous rivers of unpredictability coalesce in one place at the same time, the limits of my suppleness are challenged. I feel like bursting. And I do. I burst out of this situation where my reflection reflects another reflection. I burst out of this house where I am essentially content, but the marvel of the unknown starts to breathe heavy on my neck. I enter the world outside the house, where the streets accept me as a random element with no clear destination. I burst forward. I flow unanchored.

With my eyes closed, I take small steps in this outside world while feeling the walls and the trees with my hands. I do not want to be guided. I want the absence of light and the peace and quiet that absence evokes. At this moment, I need to vacate my mind and disrupt all connections with my own self. And this is how I usher the silence, the emptiness. I remain calm, calm, calmer... A year or one second later, upon opening my eyes again, I find myself standing in front of the redolent wound. I feel the same urgency as I once did. I am compelled to turn my back on the world as I know it. And without any hesitation, I remain within the realm of the unknown.

Part Three:

THE NAKEDNESS

Behind me, the nefarious wound stretches as long as my eyes can see. It was not cut with a knife, for its edges are irregular. It must have been carved by opposing forces, of time, of alternative lives. I cannot regard into its depths. I get scared. Better for me to create a large distance between the wound and myself. Better for me to take cover. I turn my back on the wound and what comes about is entirely in front of me. I welcome the nudity of this moment.

The street signs ignore my apparition as a person and point in no direction. They baptize streets with names that have no meaning to me. Although the colors of the buildings and their shapes are familiar, the air engulfing my body is dense with unfamiliarity. Could it be that this place is part of only a part of me? There is a danger in not knowing the deepest caverns of our selves. But who gets to venture that far?

Nothing as exciting as the now stripped of its ballast. I will not be tipping over. I can certainly move in this now world without the fear of instability. In the end, the sense of safety and control is only an illusion. I am not seeking that illusion. I am content with what there is in front of me. And thus, I march ahead under the shade of noble trees. At first, the need to move seems imminent, a desire that needs satiation. But as I become more and more comfortable with not heading in any particular di-rection, I consider the possibility of throwing an anchor and floating on this sea of time.

I simply slow my pace until I come to a full stop, the precise spot on the surface of the earth having no importance. I choose to stand because it gives me a higher point of view from where to observe the world spinning around me. Abandoning all need to interact with the reality that impacts me at this moment, I become an inheritor and accept whatever happens. Life seems to be happening, for I see people of all ages moving in all directions. I assume they all have a purpose, even if they do not know what the real purpose is. Underneath my feet, the world must be turning. This movement generates a gentle breeze that feels reassuring. I also wonder if the world itself knows its purpose. If it knew, I imagine it would be frightening. Maybe the breeze is meant to attenuate the harshness, the inhuman realities tied around the world's neck.

Existing as a hovering entity seems very simple. All I am doing is being. What is complicated is to actually know where and when I am doing the being. Away from the wound, that is clear. Also, away from what felt familiar to me. Away from that face with no expression, from the music of my flute, from the house that protects me. If, indeed, I am away from all of that. Then there is the question of time. One that I may not want to elucidate.

In the span of an indeterminate number of minutes, I experience what it feels to be a passive observer. The convoluted interactions taking place among people are formidable. Interestingly, certain gestures are repeated by diverse people with no apparent relation to each other, like waving goodbye or covering the bright sun with the palm of the hand. These must be the repertoire of core gestures shared by the masses. Then, occasionally, I observe a particular and idiosyncratic gesture that seems to belong to a single person, like an old woman kissing a flower. If the shared gestures are the result of a common cultural experience, then the idiosyncratic ones need to be further explained. I wonder, then, if those people who behave in odd ways represent the ultimate example of individual freedom. I gesture; therefore, I am. Mimicking may be a great way to learn when we are children, but it may hinder our individual freedom. I cannot consider myself a very free person because I do not remember my childhood. And maybe all my gestures are copies of the gestures of others.

I continue to observe as people go about their lives in front of me. To welcome the improbable, I begin to pay more attention to those people displaying idiosyncratic gestures. The wilder they are, the more intriguing to me, and the more promising. Then a man comes down the street who appears to be walking over clouds. His steps are so weightless and soft, so clean. His tempo is perfect: not too hurried, but not too sluggish either. He must possess a certain degree of freedom. He cannot be a derivative of another person. I regard this man as he approaches the spot where I stand. And after he passes by me, I begin to follow him in silence.

Where this man is going, I cannot tell, but he may be heading where clouds abound. I do not feel any apprehension within me, so I gather he must be walking away from the wound. That is reassuring. To prevent my presence from derailing his trajectory, I must keep a safe distance. I want him to walk in complete freedom. I want that freedom to lead my own walk. I want him to walk over the clouds.

After a serpentine trajectory which I could not possibly repeat, he walks right in front of a house that seems like my house. I am not certain of the reality of this place, but the number "3" on the door offers a certain degree of familiarity. Then the clouds come together to welcome my arrival. I like to walk on them; I like to feel them under my own feet. Unaware of my reality, the man keeps on walking. His steps are so weightless.

My initial impulse is to enter the house at once. But I resist. Instead, I conduct a visual inventory of the façade in search for any changes or deviations from the image of my house originally stored in my mind. Everything looks the same as it ever was. Either this is the same house, or it is a perfect copy. The problem is that if I use the image in my mind as a point of reference, I would then be comparing the house in front of me with a copy of the house and not with the house itself. If a copy is faithful to another copy, does that eliminate the need for the real object? What would be the point of safeguarding reality? Better to accept this house as it is.

I feel content to stand in front of my house. I also feel content to open the door and let myself inside. And just as I feel the warmth emanating from the walls, I start looking for traces of the woman with no expression. She may be in the patio soaking in the abundant freedom, or she may be rehearsing her reflection behind abstractions, or she may not be anywhere around here. Remaining very quiet, I listen for her chanting: nothing, only silence. Yes, I can go searching for her all over the house. But what would happen if I actually find her? Even worse, what would happen if I do not find her at all?

I move close to the window to regard the world outside. From this point of view, the world seems so small, unimportant, constrained. Whereas, when I walk outside, the immensity of the world is almost unbearable. It may be more prudent to see the world through a window, to frame its vast possibilities. That is what we do when we look through a person's eyes; we frame the vastness of the mind. And perhaps that is why the woman with no expression has vacuous eyes. She may not want to be classified and reduced. Her mind refuses framing. The same happens with her chant. If it contained identifiable words, I would have deciphered her full story. By not saying anything, she allows for everything.

Through the window frame, I see several trees in the process of letting their leaves fall. They do that with abandon, unafraid of becoming naked. The leaves do not seem to care; they let the wind take them where it wishes. I should do like the trees and abandon my preconceptions. Shed all mechanized thoughts until just the naked trunk remains. At the appropriate time, new leaves will spring up. So perhaps I should not search for the woman with no expression, she will emerge. I should not be concerned with my flute; the music will find me. I should disregard the world outside; it will still be there for me. I should just exist, period.

Should I look for my wine in the kitchen? That would be pure existence, ancient, deliberately conceived to link humans with their ancestors. If Odysseus drunk wine thousands of years ago, even if he was only a myth, he certainly liberated the gesture for generations to carry forward. When I raise a glass, is it me who performs the gesture, or is it the embodiment of the original gesture forged in ancient times? But I do not mix my wine with water, nor do I drink from golden goblets, so my gesture is mine, but not entirely unique. I have blood in my veins. But whose blood is it? Where did it come from?

If we cannot be originators, what are we then? Mere forms containing a vital essence that flows through time? I refuse not to be who I am, even if who I am is not completely clear. Even if I exist in multiples, yes, there must be a heritage embedded in every one of our cells. But that heritage has been exposed to hard blows, executions, tempests, and oblivion. All those forces molded this abstruse self of mine. Let me then go for the wine and drink it as myself in camaraderie with Odysseus and those who followed in his steps.

On my way to the kitchen, I pass by the French doors preventing the patio from invading the house. I can feel the tension. The high pressure of freedom makes the glass pieces in the French door bulge slightly inward. I am afraid they will burst. If they were to burst, freedom would flood the entire house, reaching as high as the candelabra. Never before have I felt the discrepancy between the inner and the outer freedom pressure. Maybe I have been complacent.

I consider ignoring the bulging doors and continue in search of the immemorial glass of wine. But I get the sense that something magnanimous is happening. I cannot believe this is only about freedom. With caution, I approach the French doors, turn the doorknob counterclockwise, and very slowly create a vertical sliver opening to the patio. What enters into the house is a torrent, not made of freedom, but of the melodic chant produced by the woman with no expression. Her voice raises a storm that infiltrates the house. Everything rattles, everything shakes. And not being capable of holding the pressure any longer, I let go of the doors and brace myself.

This chant is as ancient as our need for freedom, as the wine Odysseus offered me, as the sense of marvel I feel when I see the woman standing in the center of the patio. She appears to be completely oblivious of the energy she projects. She must be existing in a moment out of time. She must be on the edge of her own precipice. I suspect she wants me to witness her private miracle. Perhaps she wants me to feel like a voyeur, watching as she explores the depths of her void. Like she watched over me when I contemplated my reflected abstraction inside the painting. What are we becoming to each other?

Not only does the music enter into every crease of the house, but it also scurries through my ears and lodges itself inside my auditory cortex. And once in control of that domain, it begins to reorient cells and form novel neural connections. With the tingling of my brain cells, I begin to obtain a better image of this woman. But as I approach what seems like a clearer vision of her face, new musical notes dislodge the image and mystify everything. I feel as if her image comes in and out of focus in rhythm with her melody. I could try to control the process, but to what avail? So, I encourage the interlude between the chant and my brain. I welcome the visual interplay between her face and the unknown. I just exist in this irregular moment and accept it as mine.

When the storm settles, and the musical vibrations attenuate, I manage to go through the French doors and enter the patio. I expect freedom to welcome me. I also expect to come face-to-face with her, with her chant. All the flowers are here, all the space. But when I search for her presence, what I find is an absence. She is not present in the patio, at least not materially. I am certain to have seen her image. And clearly, I heard her voice. However, what remains of the woman is the idea of having seen and heard her. Nothing more. My brain, nonetheless, retains the imprint of the musical notes in the form of new connections.

I can only see what I can see and hear what I can hear. I can always imagine something else not present in front of me, perhaps devoid of existence. I can entertain the possibility of otherness. But when the other is so palpable—and beautiful—how could it not be entirely present? How do we decide what touches us deeply? Whatever is palpable, or whatever has a stronger impact? Does my brain care for the source of the sensation, or is my brain satisfied with the sensation itself, regardless of its origin? This I ponder as I reach out with my hand and touch nothing.

#

In this house of mine, there is a flute of mine. If the space containing me this very moment contains all the components of my house as well, then my flute has to be somewhere around here. I do not believe that with certainty, but I do have the suspicion that this world is ordered in a similar way to the world I have known thus far. That does not mean that this is my world, but who am I to doubt that it is not?

The first room that I enter has an impressive mahogany bookshelf housing row upon row of books in various languages. Some rows are dedicated to literature, others to atlases and maps, several rows contain books on art, a few others are devoted to music. Then there is an entire section on mythology, mysticism, and everything that cannot be touched. Tempted as I am to verify that these are indeed the books I have read over many years, I refrain from opening a single one of them. That is a concern for another time. I came into this room looking for my flute, and I ought to fulfill that mission. I just came from a patio full of music and empty of words. And toward music, I oscillate.

In front of the massive bookshelf, there is a desk and a chair. In a corner of the room, I see a divan and a reading lamp. I imagine my flute could be waiting for me in this room. But there is no flute to be found. The spirit of words is what reigns here, but not the spirit of music. So, I leave this room behind, knowing that I will have to return when in need of words.

I then glide into another room I seem to recognize. And leaning against the wall, there is a wooden flute I may have played before. This flute is identical to a flute I once played in a room similar to this, and that flute was identical to the one I used to play. Or, perhaps, all the flutes are the same flute. I may just be encountering the one and only flute in what appears to be dissimilar but very related places. Regardless of which flute this may be, I am intent on playing it.

I lift the wooden flute, and my fingers find the holes with the intuition of flying bats. I recognize the weight of the wood and the aroma under my nose. I take a deep breath, and before I blow into the flute, I arrest all efforts. I was about to play notes I remember as if I needed to talk to the flute or to talk to myself. This is not the moment for words. What matters now is to orchestrate a musical response to the wordless chant of the woman. She touched me with her melody in the patio; I should be able to touch her in the same way —without words.

I set the stage for a fateful encounter with the notes. I have a sense of what I might play, but I do not know what I will play. The notes will need to emerge from the white center of me. I will summon them, but I will not direct them. This is not the time for shepherding; this is the time for letting loose. So, I blow into the flute and let my fingers dance at will.

In their randomness, the notes aggregate and form a set of beautiful phrases. The resulting melody has no resemblance to any other melody I may recall. It defies my memory and knowledge of known rhythms. I allow it to flow because it seems to ask for existence. In this very moment, my intention and intuition are fused. As I listen to myself playing, I cannot recognize my own musical style. It seems as if another person is playing the flute through me. Or, perhaps, I am listening to myself playing from another reality I have yet to master. The melody then grows and begins to spill out of the room into the rest of the house. The face of this melody is as inscrutable as the face of the woman. They both express an inner richness without forming a single exterior wrinkle. And the less control I exercise in my playing, the richer the melody, the grander the volume, the more satisfying.

Still playing, still wanting to touch the woman with my melody, I walk out of the room where I found the flute and enter the main corridor of the house. Here the melody assumes an entirely different characteristic. A chromatic transposition creates a sonority equivalent to the Phrygian mode the woman used in her chant. Intuitively, my fingers want to touch her without hands, only with improvised notes.

At the end of the corridor, the French doors are still open. I know the patio waits for me on the other side. The woman may be standing in the center of the patio. She may be listening to the flowers or to my melody. But just as well, she may still be completely absent. That is the only reality, the not knowing.

Entirely shrouded in my melody, I advance toward the patio. Walking through the French doors with my flute is not an obligation. It is a choice. But a choice I want to make. And as I do so, the sweet sense of freedom comes to greet me. The woman with no expression, however, does not do the same. Her physical absence is magnanimous. Accepting this imminent reality, I continue to improvise with my flute. My melody goes up into the sky; it ascends and expands. In the vastness of the sky, my melody finds the vestiges of her chant still vibrating and resounding. The two Phrygian modes recognize each other. Unafraid, they intertwine and continue to ascend and expand together—an extemporaneous touch without fingers or words.

On this irrevocable ground, I remain, imagining what the horizon looks like from the heights of my melody. I wonder if the melody enjoys a view of the sea. I know the melody will travel forever, evolving, and reinventing itself. To produce something as eternal and as intangible brings me tremendous joy. Not only am I joyous, but free and unencumbered. I take care to place the flute in a dry corner of the patio and regard the height of the wall that separates the patio from the outside world. Absolutely scalable, I have seen cats do the trick. I am not vaulting over the wall; I just need to get on top of it. If the music is fearless, I can be fearless as well.

I step back to create enough space for me to run. With sufficient speed, I should be able to fling myself up and reach the top of the wall with one or both hands. Once dangling, I could swing my legs and straddle the wall. From there, I can enter the world outside. I could also avoid this acrobatic proposal and exit through the front door of the house. But that is not the way my melody found her melody. I want to do as the music did, I am simply trusting my nature.

I do get the speed that I need. I do jump as high as I can. I manage to grab the top of the wall from where I now hang. And with a spirited effort, I pull myself up and straddle the wall. Behind me is the patio where freedom resides. In front of me is the rest of the world. Can freedom be totally contained? Probably not, and that is why the patio is open to the sky. But freedom can be limited. This wall is a limit. Yes, I can break through the limit provided I make a strong effort and take the necessary risks. Sitting on top of the limit itself gives me a fresh perspective. The rest of the world seems to exist. And somewhere out there, there is a dividing wound. I scan the horizon, but my eyes cannot see it.

With the same delicacy as when I climbed, I let my body hang on the outside of the wall. It seems the distance between my feet and the ground is much larger on this side. That is my reality now, and I accept it. I will need to let go of my hands and assimilate the impact of the fall as best I can. I am afraid of letting go, for I may get hurt. But if I do not let go, I would be hanging on to a perceived limit. And climbing back up is not an option I want to take. So, I just let go of the wall and fall freely to the ground. At the moment of impact, I let my legs absorb the brunt of the force, then I roll over the ground and enter the world outside.

This must be how a baby feels when entering the world. A traumatic experience, thus the crying. I have no reason for crying since I did not get hurt. But the abruptness of the entrance is nonetheless traumatic. And like a baby, I have no control over the world that opens up in front of me. I quickly realize that the act of rolling on the ground provides a swift change in my point of view. In the process of rolling, I got the sensation the world was turning when the one turning was me. If I were to repeat the experience, the world would be changing with each individual roll, and so would my perception of reality. To test the potential of this phenomenon, I kneel on the ground and bend forward until the top of my head touches the ground. Then I push with my feet until I roll over my back and come to a sitting position. The world has changed. Not a formidable change, but sufficient to alter my perception. I wonder if reversing the experience would bring me back to my previous point of view. But how does one roll back? Even if I did, nothing would guarantee that the previous point of view would still be there waiting for me.

I get back on my feet and look around. A few people walk by but seem oblivious to my antics. Perhaps they see me as an overgrown child, or as an adult with childish ways. As I walk down the street, an unsettling familiarity invades my awareness. Unsettling because what I see seems utterly familiar, but not enough to make it a true known. I stop for a moment to clarify if the assembly of houses and street signs is a real place or a place I recognize as almost real. Impossible to tell. Then

I get on my knees and try a simple roll on the ground. And as I expected, the world transforms in front of me. I manage to defamiliarize my surroundings. Attracted by the freshness of my reality, I continue to walk down the street.

After a few blocks of nothing other than unfamiliarity, I am assaulted by the smell of decay. An acrid smell that sits on the air and refuses to move. I cannot tell what the source is. Across the street, a little boy and his dog play as if the smell did not bother them. Maybe they have gotten used to smelling this miasmatic air. But this is unfamiliar to me and very repugnant. I accelerate my pace and make a few turns right and left. The smell seems to follow me, or I may be entering deeper into its territory, I do not know. I stand still and hold my breath for as long as I can. How long could my body go without oxygen? Would I be able to erase the memory of the smell? My body revolts. Gasping for air, I then take a deep breath. The stench is still there. I begin to run. I run faster. And the unfamiliarity of the streets comes to an abrupt end when the dividing wound opens up in front of me. I recognize the wound I have previously crossed, but it has changed. It has begun to decompose. In front of me: rotten flesh, pure cadaverine.

There are moments when the world foists on us an unbearable reality. When we are pummeled by forces out of our control, this is one of those moments. I will not accept this reality as legitimate and will not integrate it into myself. Nothing compels me to be that passive. So, I kneel on the ground and roll away from the pestilent wound. Everything begins to shift. The world tilts. I roll once again with even more force. Behind me, the wound seems now vertical, now horizontal, now jagged. I string one roll with another, and like a rolling stone, my body tumbles over the ground for what seems a great distance. The unknown vector of my movement continues until I come to the edge of the sea. Here I stop rolling, for there is no purpose in joining the sea.

I plant my two feet on the sand and try to stand up. At first, the horizon refuses to level out. It undulates as if the water and the sky were cavorting with each other. I close my eyes to eliminate all visual references, but the darkness inside spins in a shapeless space. Calm. Calm, there is no use in desperation; time will come to my rescue. And it does. A few minutes later, I open my eyes, and the horizon appears docile, the sea and the sky in peaceful and perfect harmony. To my delight, the wound and the stench are no longer. This altered reality is of my own creation, even if only partially. I set my body in a random tumbling motion, and the world lost its hold on me.

The sea deserves my deepest admiration. It lies unperturbed on its bed of sand, extending as wide and far as it wishes. The wind, no matter how strong, can only roughen its surface, leaving its depths unscathed. We may create memories of a particular sea, at a particular time, but the sea does not remember us. The sea does not take offense. We can carve its back with the keel of a boat, and it will remain quiet, healing as soon as the boat moves on. It is supple, the sea, and lets the moon pull it away from the shores, or toward them. It does not kill, but we can die in its depths because of our own foolishness. That sea in front of me already existed before I could even dream of my own existence.

And there it is, the sea, contemplating my inconsequential reality. If it were to talk to me, it would probably tell me not to fear chaos. That changes come and go, like the waves on its surface. That I should not worry about time, for there is no beginning or end to it. That our bodies do not belong only to us for others can enter it. That we all harbor a beautiful light as well as deep darkness. That at some point, there is stillness to be had.

#

Away from the sea, an immense expanse of land awaits me. I know I belong to one territory or another. But I do not know to which one precisely. Even if I get the sensation that I am floating over the earth, over this reality, I know I have touched the ground before. I could not just have started being yesterday, or today. My essence, my humanity, must have been conceived at some point. I may not have evolved linearly, but I have evolved, albeit randomly.

If my belonging has been thrown into disarray as a result of the vicissitudes of time, then I should be free to choose any territory of my liking to belong to. For example, this semi-familiar neighborhood is a good candidate. Likewise, I could walk for a thousand kilometers to find a new territory and make it my abode. The only problem is that belonging implies a certain consistency and permanence. I am already suspect of time. As of permanence, I cannot imagine any other concept as porous as that.

The problem may reside in the physical nature of our movement over the earth. With every step, we acquire a certain confirmation of our presence. We establish a physical connection with the world, with the ground underneath our feet. That world, then, may place a claim on our existence. But we keep on walking our entire lives, establishing new connections with every step, and severing those connections as we move on. We are always eradicating ourselves.

There is that house somewhere around here that feels like home. At the same time, even when I am inside of it, the house fails to ground me completely. I may have entered and exited the house a thousand times. And with every entry, I harmonize, mostly. But with every exit, I extricate myself. That house contains me as much as any other territory in the world. Maybe if I had memories buried in that patio, the sense of belonging would be stronger. But just as permanence, memories are rather porous.

I do walk ahead and carve through the territory in front of me. I consider floating immaterially, like a shadow. But my corporeal reality does not permit that. I resort to putting aside all expectations so I can easily glide and avoid shallow belongings. The houses and dogs pass by me without attempting to hang on or to claim acquaintance. Not relating is not belonging, and without talking to anyone or petting any animal, I advance through the streets in the perceived direction of the house that could be mine.

Along the way, I confront what appears to be a sudden change in temperature. What felt like a comfortable April morning has turned into a torrid July afternoon. The wind has not changed its direction or speed, nor has it rained. So, this change must be my bodily response to unacceptable belongings. I must be getting awfully close to that house. I can sense it. I should admit that I want to enter that house and search for the woman with no expression. Even if encountering her threatens me with the danger of belonging.

Ushered by the afternoon heat, I soon come to stand once again in front of the house. It looks exactly as it did the previous time when I stood in front of it. The number "3" is there to confirm the address. Why would it change, this house? The answer ought to be that the house would not change on its own, that the people that inhabit the house are the ones that change continuously.

The veracity of that answer is challenged by what develops in front of my eyes. Through the windows of the house, I see the silhouette of a man and a woman facing each other. It is not clear to me if they are talking or just contemplating each other. From where I stand, I cannot distinguish their faces. They disappear from one window, and soon enough they reemerge in another window. I wonder who inhabits this house that could be mine. It is entirely possible that what I am now seeing is nothing but the memory of myself and the woman with no expression. I have stood facing her without saying a word. People on the street would have certainly seen our silhouettes. Maybe the arrow of time is playing tricks on me.

I try to listen for their words, but I hear nothing. I try to listen for her chant or my flute music, but no melody comes to my ears. The only thing that I hear is the sweat beading on my forehead in this torrid afternoon. Then the silhouettes vanish from the window, and no other form comes to replace them. Have they disappeared or is it time that shifted its flow? I cannot tell. I start walking around the house, hoping to catch a glimpse of the silhouettes again, perhaps hoping to encounter my own memories. But looking into the house from all possible angles yields nothing other than empty rooms that I barely recognize.

Following the perimeter of the house brings me to the wall that separates the patio from the outside world.

This is the frontier I fringed to land in this reality. As I stand regarding the wall, the freedom oozing out of the patio feels exquisitely refreshing. I should be able to reverse the process and reinsert myself inside of the house by way of the patio. The only thing that gets on my way is the wall, which seems much taller from this side. But perhaps the wall is not taller. It may appear that way due to its function as a barrier, safekeeping my vulnerabilities, guarding her chant, and my music. I decide to attempt the same acrobatic feat that worked once before. Without hesitation, I run as fast as I can toward the wall and leap up in the air. I barely manage to grab the top of the wall. Trusting myself, I swing my legs and straddle the wall. This time, the rest of the world is behind me. In front of me is the patio where freedom resides.

The patio seems to welcome my return, for it does not change its mood when I land on the ground. The flowers continue to exude their respective fragrances. I feel a certain peace that may or may not be related to a sense of belonging. But that is not important at this moment. What matters now is to search for her chant, that ephemeral melody imbued with a meaning I have yet to decipher. I see my flute, resting silently in a corner of the patio. If I were to play the flute, I would be calling her. In seeking her that way, I may inadvertently lose her. In reaching, I would be pushing away. I would fail in my efforts to cause her appearance. She would need to occur on her own.

Thus, I decide not to decide anything. I will just rest in the patio and allow for reality to reveal itself to me. Of course, I am assuming that reality feels an obligation to reveal itself. What if reality just happens without taking me into consideration? Reality has no need for me; it can exist on its own. If I were to ignore reality, and reality did the same with me, then what happens is irrelevant as far as it concerns me. So, I find myself in this patio just being—not a bad place to be. The sense of freedom is exquisite, and the flowers beautiful. However, the only thing missing is a sense of otherness—otherness as it relates to another individual. And the lack of otherness does not imply loneliness, for I do not feel lonely. Perhaps the problem is that just being is not sufficient. Or perhaps I am formulating excuses to justify my desire to search after her.

While in the midst of doing nothing but thinking, I hear the chirping sound of a few birds that come to visit the patio. Little black birds these are, traveling from one land to another, looking for food and shelter. They must have alerted their comrades because, all of a sudden, hundreds of these creatures invade the patio. They talk to each other, they chirp. And the sound is strident enough to arrest my thought process. I listen to them, but I cannot understand what they say to each other or to me. I was not expecting them, and they were not expecting me either. Chance brought us together. They are totally free, the little black birds. But they are searching, nonetheless. They fly freely in search of some instinctual need. They follow a path they did not know they were following. Would that be chance after all? To act without knowing we are following a script. I clap my hands loudly. All the birds fly away in the same direction.

The appropriate thing to do at this moment would be to stop hovering over time and my own consciousness. So, I abandon my preoccupations with the birds and breach the French doors. Inside the house, the air feels stagnant. I cannot tell if the house has been closed for a long time or if I am on the brink of a memory. I believe this is the house from which I left not too long ago in search of her chant and freedom. A reverse trajectory, however, does not guarantee a return to the point of origin. The origin is nothing but an agreement about the precise coordinates where place and time intersect. I have little faith in the arrow of time. As for place, nothing seems to remain where we think it is as a result of displacement, or of the inherent mutability of our reality.

Walking down the corridor in search of fresh air brings me face-to-face with a framed photograph hanging on a large and otherwise empty wall. It is the black and white portrait of a boy I do not recognize. This portrait must have a special meaning; otherwise, why would it be hanging in the middle of this wall? Not only do I not recognize the child, but if this is indeed my house, then I do not recall hanging the picture. That is entirely possible, and perhaps even desirable.

I observe the image of the boy with the utmost attention. I look at his eyes, at his mouth. The features reveal nothing familiar to me. The boy seems to be looking directly at the person holding the camera. He seems to be asking a question. But what question? He could be asking why he needs to pose for a picture. Or he could be asking what his origin is. Most likely, the answers he received were meaningless. What is not meaningless is the fact that this picture is hanging in front of me and that the air feels stagnant. Or is that meaningless as well? I can construe all sorts of explanations, and they will be as meaningless as the answers the boy received. The problem may not reside in asking these questions, but in expecting an answer.

To avoid further encounters of this kind, I think of turning the picture around to negate the image. However, I refrain myself. Turning the picture around would only remind me that I had a need to turn around such picture to avoid some discomfort. And that, as a result, would only elicit further discomfort. It may be better to allow the boy to continue looking at the camera, even if it is me at whom he is looking now. He may not know his origin, but neither do I know mine. There is no threat in his inquiring gaze. I turn my back on the boy and wash my memory of having seen him. Then I continue walking down the corridor. The air loses some of its stiffness.

The idea of wine becomes an imperative. When a

rupture is called for, wine often provides the necessary force. Having found my favorite wine in the kitchen at least once leads me to believe that I will find it again. Provided this house continues to impersonate my former house, and more importantly, that a past event augurs a similar one in the future. I find the kitchen exactly where it is supposed to be. In the kitchen, all the expected utensils are in their expected places. The only absence I register is that of my favorite wine. I search for it everywhere but find nothing. The wine glasses are present, clean, but there is no wine to fill them. I find this situation rather peculiar. Why would something become absent the moment we have a pointed need for that something? Would the wine be here in the kitchen if I had not wished to drink some of it? An affirmative answer would be devastating, for it would imply a superior conscience with the capacity to know my desires and to manipulate outcomes within my reality. For that very reason, I stop looking for the wine and try to tame my wishes.

In the kitchen sink, a single drop of water falls out of the faucet, making an almost imperceptible sound. One or two seconds later, another drop takes the leap. They seem like identical drops. As I continue to observe, it becomes evident that there is a caravan of drops going through the faucet. This must be a tribal ritual, a suicidal march. But the accumulation of individual landings creates a smooth and soothing rhythm, perfect in its tempo. I focus on the sound and allow for the rhythm to settle my mind. The only thing to expect is that a drop will fall. And unexpectedly, then, the chant of the woman with no expression emerges from somewhere inside the house and reaches my ears.

#

The voice, sublime and expressive, instills in me a sense of disequilibrium. Maybe her chant will acquire a clear meaning if I stop trying to understand it. The pure melody could exist on its own without any interpretation. The fact that she sings does not mean that she is singing for me. Perhaps what I hear is the sound of her thoughts or her memories.

Irrespective of its purpose, the melody grows inside the house. It seems to fill the cavernous rooms creating alluring reverberations. I allow myself to feel the music without investing it with meaning. And like a wave at the seashore, the melody crashes on me. I lose my sense of place, of time. All I feel are the sound vibrations that surround me. The melody transforms itself into an engulfing presence.

Once the sea recedes, I find the woman sitting in front of me; her face still an enigma. She is quiet now, dreaming perhaps, or just being. In her hands, she holds a bottle of the wine I could not find before. She must know that I was looking for it. She finds me and finds my

133

wine. I only lose myself and find nothing along the way. I am about to consider that her presence has a meaning. But I better restrain myself from finding meaning, for it only deepens the void.

This is a moment when nothing needs to be done other than to be present—allowing for the world to manifest itself is in order. And that is exactly what I do. I remain seated in front of the woman and forget that I am a musician, that I, perhaps, live in this house, that there is an infected wound somewhere in the outside world. I forget that I do not know who this woman is. And I forget that I had forgotten so much of my life.

She serves two glasses of wine. Without waiting for me, she drinks from her glass. I regard her and wonder if she likes this wine as much as I do. But that is another attempt at trying to understand her. So, I push aside my natural tendencies to unravel mysteries and try to marvel at the simple miracle of being in her presence. I raise my glass of wine and drink from it. And drop by drop the wine falls inside my body completely unmindful of its potential influence. In spite of its complexity, the wine exists without knowing about its existence. The woman exists, but she is not aware of the influence she exerts on me. In my mind, my own existence is questionable, and my influence, a mere speculation.

I believe time passes, or at least the world rotates on its axis. I know because I feel the influence of wine within me. Still facing this woman, but more at ease with myself, I consider talking to her. I could verbalize my thoughts and offer them in their naked form. What would the risk be? I am not ashamed of my doubts. But what is it that I have to say? A disarray of ill-conceived ideas? My thoughts do not have to align themselves in perfect rows and behave like sensical soldiers. Regardless, nothing in my thought process will change this situation. And in all likelihood, she may not respond to what I have to say.

Heartened, I open the floodgates and start talking. At first, the words come out garbled as if I were learning how to speak. Then I manage to form logical sentences with inconsequential meaning. Then I proceed to describe what is obvious, like the fact that we are seated in front of each other drinking wine. None of these useless words elicit a reaction from the woman. She retains her immaculate, expressionless face.

She then serves me another glass of wine. Perhaps to encourage me to continue talking, or perhaps to signal that talking is a useless exercise. To allow for either possibility, I drink half of the glass at once. To continue with my monologue, I propose various concepts: that purposefulness is only apparent, that sitting in front of each other, as we are now doing, will lead to nothing other than sitting in front of each other, that all I can hope for is for the intervention of arbitrary gods in my life but that, fortunately, or unfortunately, I do not believe in any god-like creature. I then confess that my circle of fate is broken.

After my final words, a magical silence descends over both of us. Her face, as still as the face of the moon. Confronting this implacability, I succumb to the silence. A silence that affects deeply. In the immediacy of this outer world, nothing happens—inside of me, the turning of the seas. Inside of her, the sea unfathomable. She drinks from her glass with a gesture as ancient as wine itself. She then stands in front of me. And, softly, she starts to chant in Phrygian mode.

The melody begins to flood the house once more. It reaches my ankles, my knees. It mounts and mounts. I let go of my chair and give in to the force of the melody. I am now floating on my back, the melody sustaining the entire weight of my body. I shall not resist, for there is no purpose in resisting. I simply allow for the melody to transport me where it ought to. This fluid energy may be the direct representation of her thoughts, a powerful melody capable of moving me. Or this could be the unintended consequences of a force unleashed, the raw effect of that unfathomable sea. I float, delighted.

When the melody recedes, I find myself lying on the ground, supine, and completely naked. There is no roof above me, only the sky. And no walls hug me, but an openness where trees stand in observation. I know that I am not in the house and that I am alone. I must have traveled, that is clear, but how far and for how long? Is it me who drifted, or is it the world that drifted below me?

As for my nakedness, the trees do not seem to care, for they are bare as well.

In the distance, the shape of a person materializes. Someone very small, or a child perhaps, walks in my direction. As the shape gets closer, I recognize the young girl carrying her cat. Her radiant smile, I remember. I realize that if she gets any closer, she would come across my nakedness. Mortified, I roll over the ground and hide behind one of the naked trees.

She must have noticed something because she changes her direction and heads directly toward the tree covering my body. With no other place to go, I stand still and hope the girl will just walk by and disappear. But she does not do that. Instead, she walks all the way up to the tree and stops on the opposite side of where I stand. She does not say a single word, nor does she take another step. Apparently, she lays the cat on the ground because the creature comes circling around the tree and then runs away to chase imaginary shadows. When the cat gets too far, she calls it by its name. She calls it "Babylos."

I am not sure that she just used that name. I am not sure that she has spoken at all. But the cat does respond and returns to the other side of the tree. Then I hear her steps as if walking away. With caution not to be seen, I look around the trunk of the tree and confirm that her little shape is effectively vanishing in the distance. She must be smiling. I am sure she is.

Wherever I may be, I could be found. People may recognize me and feel embarrassed in front of my nakedness. People that do not recognize me would also feel embarrassed. I should not be seen like this out in the world, even if this world is questionable. I may need to hide. Not hide who I am, but my nakedness. I can go from tree to tree, from one alley to another, and stay away from people's eyes until reaching the house. But where is that house of mine? In what direction?

I reflect, look at my surroundings, spot the position of the sun. The details are meager. If I were to head in any particular direction, I would be clearly guessing. I accept guessing, what is life but a guessing game? But I would prefer certitude in this naked moment. I take a deep breath. The air filtering through my nose provides an unexpected clue. Salt, sultriness, the sea…

Right above me, I can hear the fluttering leaves on the tree. I look up and observe their delicate movements and determine the direction from where the breeze is coming. That must be the afternoon inland breeze, making them dance so nervously. The sea must be lying on its back not far from here. The problem is how to stay out of sight until I reach the sea. I could deny my existence and pretend that nobody would see me as I move through the streets and alleys. But the fact of negating my existence does not guarantee that other people would do the same. People on the streets may validate my existence against my will. If they did, they would be the ones utterly bothered by my nakedness. The expression on their faces would certainly make me uncomfortable. That will force me to consider myself as a real entity in front of their eyes. That will shatter my non-existence. A relative world this is.

Once I confirm that there is nobody in the vicinity, I run as fast as I can and slide under a bush downwind from the tree where I am hiding. Not a very welcoming bush, for it has vicious thorns all over. Avoiding any contact with this prickly beast, I spot a dark alley that I can easily reach in a mad dash. I launch myself and make it to the alley unscathed. There is enough darkness here to hide my nakedness. I take a peek down the larger street where the breeze is coming from. It is virtually empty. People must be indoors having lunch, or they already know that I am coming and took cover. The fact that I do not see people does not mean they do not see me. I have never been invisible.

Little by little, I make my way down the street in pure concealment—jumping in between parked cars, receding into doorways, standing behind lampposts and garbage cans, even blending with the walls. My efforts seem to succeed, for I hear no panic screams, nor do I face any confrontation. And as I suspected, at the end of the street, I reach the edge of the sea. What remains is for me to cross the wide-open band of sand and immerse myself into the concealing waters.

Crouched, I wait for the precise moment when the

empty space becomes even emptier. That is the moment when the breeze stops, and nothing moves. Perhaps the sliver of a moment between two consecutive moments. I recognize it as soon as it arrives, and I run the last few meters and throw myself into the sea—a welcoming embrace. With my nakedness washed away, I can now calm my senses. And I do. I find peace in knowing that the sea does not care about who I am or what my reality is. The sea has its own depths to worry about.

The wind has been blowing for a while, making the sea uneasy. It grows waves on its back. I resist the push of the waves that insist on spitting me out onto the sandy shore. Sometimes I jump to keep my head above water. Other times I submerge myself and wait for the wave to crest over me. This bobbing up and down is somewhat disorienting. I hear a mixture of sounds—the slapping of the waves, the sharp cry of the seagulls, the wind whistling. Then there are the voices of those who drowned a long time ago. In the midst of the commotion, I hear Babylos calling himself. His voice sounds far and choked. I look around me in all directions—nothing but the boiling sea, no boats, no bodies.

I could easily join the body of the sea. By not countering its force, I could float and be carried where the sea may take me. I may not arrive alive, but I would arrive. What do I stand to lose? I am already naked and dispossessed. As I consider these thoughts, a wave rolls over me, and I swallow a good amount of seawater. I struggle for air. In desperation, my body takes control and mounts a frantic response. My arms start flailing, and my legs thrash violently. This is not my mind in control but my brainstem. Then another savage wave comes around and sends me flipping over my head and onto the shore. Without intending, the sea has rejected me.

Lying naked on the shore, I hear the rage of the waves. I hear the seagulls laughing. I think I hear the chant of that mysterious woman coming from somewhere far away. All external bearings for my thoughts are now silent as if all worries have been erased. To re-integrate myself into the flow of my adopted reality, I must proceed with care. I must be re-born. I first need to give a shape to my body. To accomplish this, I resort to rolling on the sand over and over until my entire body is crusted with a thick layer of wet sand. Inside the sandy shell, I am still naked. But to the observing eyes of the world, I have a shape and maybe even intentions.

If the chant I barely distinguish belongs to the expressionless woman, then my reality is somewhere in the vicinity. I should be able to reinsert myself into its flow. I admit that following the chant would be an intentional and a questionable act. But if I do, at some point, I will intersect that fleeting reality of mine.

#

In principle, there can only be one sea, one house

of mine, and one village. There could be many women, but only one lacking facial expression. There are innumerable melodies, but the fashion in which I relate to them is uniquely mine. In spite of these and many other essential singularities, I seem to navigate through a sea of pluralities. This, a completely acceptable reality given the porous nature of our self-imposed limitations. But when I confront the plethora of possibilities in front of me, I am forced to consider myself as a honeycombed individual where many cells of my own being remain unexplored.

I decide not to fret with the ignored. Even if the streets of this village resist full recognition, I will traverse them in peace, ready to accept that I may be retracing my own steps. A gesture, even if ancient, is reborn as it is repeated, for the person who acts on it has changed with the passage of time. And time is something that eludes my understanding, which makes the proposition untenable. Better, then, to walk trusting my senses and the power of irregularities.

Interestingly, with every step I take, the melodious chant of the woman seems to get marginally louder. I walk ahead without making a conscious choice of direction. When I stop, it seems to me the chant of the woman is indeed louder. I wonder if walking toward her is volitional even when the choices I make are null. Or perhaps she is not singing at all, and what I think I hear is an augmented anticipation inside of me. That would be an interesting irregularity.

In the course of this improbable walk, I see the silhouette of an old man approaching me from a distant point. As we walk toward each other, I recognize him as the old man who came unannounced into the house and shared a glass of wine with me. We stop in front of each other. The mutual scrutiny confirms that he is that old man. However, he does not seem to recognize me. Maybe my sand-encrusted body confuses him. At first, we both stay silent while processing the meaning of this encounter.

The old man contemplates my figure and the trees around him, and as he did the previous time, he begins to talk about the vicissitudes of time. I listen attentively because his words may contain a meaning I failed to capture in our previous meeting. He embarks on a discourse about change. He warns me not to believe that permanence is superior to change. That the foundations of the world are clearly not immutable, that nothing is as real as multiplicity and motion. He then takes a pause and studies my face and my body with a puncturing tenacity. He then concludes by saying that I have changed only slightly even though he is not sure he has ever seen me before. After those words, he takes leave and does not look back.

At once, I try to listen again to the melodious chant that brought me to this juncture of time and place. I hear nothing. Where could the chant have gone? If what I was hearing was an augmented anticipation, then the chant should be resonating loud and clear, for I sense a deep need to arrive at the house. I close my eyes and turn all my attention to the sounds around me. The leaves fluttering, the grass blades quivering, but not a single note in Phrygian mode. I can imagine the melody and source it from inside my mind. But that would not be her chant; that would be a mere simulacrum.

Without sonic orientation, I find myself at the crux of multiple routes. From this point, I count 360 uncrossing pathways. To follow one is not to follow another. To follow all of them would make me turn in concentric circles. I look for clues to help me guide my course. Yes, there are houses and street signs; there are people on the sidewalks. But no iteration of these elements indicates a firm course. Perhaps the idea of choosing a particular course is irrelevant because all courses will inevitably bring me to the house, or to the contrary, none of them will.

So, I decide to create a pattern of unrelated turns that would guarantee a haphazard march. A right turn follows a left turn, sometimes. At other times, I turn left after having turned left already, but only if there is a bird in sight. In the case of a 4-way crossing, I follow the street that reminds me of my childhood. But remembering so little of my childhood renders that choice a guessing game. Nevertheless, with that set of rules as a guiding plan, I advance through this village. After walking for some time, I confirm that the rules generate a perfectly indeterminate pattern, and I feel free.

Then comes a cool breeze, and the sun loses some of its luminosity. A few clouds begin to crowd together. The color gray enters the theatre of the sky—a typical afternoon for a sea village. I welcome the change in weather as I welcome a change of mind. What I do not welcome are the raindrops that begin to fall over me. First, they are light and uninteresting. But soon, the raindrops begin to grow and fall with more force over my sand-encrusted body. Gradually, the moist sand begins to loosen its grip on my skin. It starts to melt away from my body. What emerges, then, is the same nakedness I tried to abscond before.

Soon I find myself wet and bare without really knowing where I am—a situation not caused by design, nor by consequence. What happens now happens. Like I walk into the streets or it rains when water falls from the sky. This simplicity is as clear to me as the number "3" that materializes this very instant at the entrance of the house in front of me.

For not being inevitable, this recurrent encounter with the house that could be my house is rather formidable. In the spirit of continuous acceptance, I acquiesce to my reality as an apparent returner. Apparent, because I may not be returning *per se*, but continuing on a cyclical and perhaps parallel path towards the unknown. I expect this house to contain the same elements it contained when I found myself away from it and naked on the ground. I stand here naked, so there may be a link between then and now.

Before I let myself into the house, I must come to terms with various possibilities that may ensue. First, the woman without expression may not be present in the house. She may be completely absent. In such case, the only way to conjure her presence is by way of my memory. That would be utterly disappointing, given the natural fallibility of my memory. A second possibility could be that she is in the house indeed. That would not be disappointing but rather challenging. I would need to reconcile my desire to touch her with my desire to decipher the meaning of her chant. Somehow, I sense those are mutually exclusive propositions. Or, perhaps, I see them as opposites because such strategy protects me against my own instincts. Another possibility could be that the woman has acquired a facial expression but lost her chant. That would be devastating, and I refuse to consider that scenario. The truth, however, is that I can imagine a thousand possibilities, and none will turn out as conceived. So, I enter the house.

Nothing inside the house seems to have changed. I wonder if time has taken the time to visit, or has it ignored this house. Inside the kitchen, the two wine glasses contain their wine—a profoundly reassuring image. The corridor contains the same air as before. The strange painting still hangs on the wall. I look through the French doors and see my flute resting placidly out in the patio. I dare not enter the other rooms. Clearly not the one where I saw that book. No, not that room.

I conclude that this is the house where I last heard the chant. The phenomenon is not under my control. The woman with no expression decides the fate of her own singing. It is up to her to compose the chant and project her voice. If for some reason, I elicit in her a desire to express her thoughts and feelings by means of her voice, I would have to admit that I am ignorant of how I could accomplish such a feat. Around her, I am only expectant. Her actions belong to her, even if they respond to my presence. My presence, however, could inadvertently reflect her lack of expression. She may see her own barrenness projected unto me. She could also be singing to herself. She could be using this house as an echo chamber to project her feelings and render her emotions accessible. My presence here may be just an accident.

Clearly, I cannot wish her into being. This sense of powerlessness provides me with a kind of freedom I value. I could easily continue to inhabit this house and let the chant come and go as it pleases. The natural order of things would take care of how everything will transpire. On the other hand, I could try to intervene by alluring her to appear and produce her chant. A pretentious idea for arbitrary gods would intervene to throw everything in disarray. But there is my own music. The music of the flute with which she already communed.

In haste, I breach the French doors and enter the open patio. There is my flute, resting among the clouds of freedom. The nature of the flute is freedom itself, and for that reason, it seems so at ease in this patio. I reach for the flute and consider playing a simple melody in Phrygian mode. But I place my intentions on hold because that would be a direct plea for her appearance. Such a purposeful scheme is only bound to fail. I must play unbound, letting the music come to life as it will. It was in this patio where our sounds intertwined with each other. If I were to play in this very spot, I would be forcing an occurrence.

I leave the patio behind, with its freedom and flowers, and re-enter the house with my flute. I do not want to make another choice. I will not start playing until I am certain I have no reason to play anything. I will float until the right moment becomes evident. In the midst of this unhooking, I find myself inside the kitchen where the two glasses of wine are still recumbent on the table. I sample the wine again. Good wine, indeed, my favorite. I allow for the wine to do what it needs to do. And once I feel comfortable and disentangled from any expectations, I bring the flute to my lips.

The first few notes show no promise, unrelated, uninteresting. The next progression of notes assumes a barely likable shape. But the rhythm has an uncomfortable predictability. I drink some more of the good wine. Then

I just play the flute without wanting to play anything. This time the notes cavort with each other, they frolic in the air. In the act of playing, I forget that I am playing. As for the melody I produce, I have no idea; it simply takes the shape it needs to. Like this, I go on, sourcing notes out of the air inside my lungs. After a while, I rest and drink some more of the wine. I feel ample and free, even content. The music, although it resonates loud and clear, remains unanswered. No chant comes to join with it. The woman fails to materialize.

The sense of disappointment I now feel implies an unrealized expectation. The mental image of her chant responding to my music is an invention of mine. I installed that image inside my mind and gave it credence. Also, assuming that having shared this wine with her in the past would have favored a future encounter around wine consumption is nothing but an artifice. There is nothing to expect; there has never been. I drink another glass of wine to that consideration.

With no desire for resting in the kitchen any longer, or drinking any more wine, I step out into the corridor to take my chances there. As before, the air in the corridor seems to stay still. Reassured by the steadiness of the moment, I feel free to wander around the house. Without any premeditation, the wandering brings me once again in front of the half-open door. Behind it, I am almost certain that the book is still there. However, the book cannot be waiting for me, for it has no mind. Any apprehension I feel about re-encountering the book is another invention of mine. This pattern of fabricated expectations worries me deeply. It allows for an imaginary reality to penetrate my awareness and compete with the reality in front of my eyes—a treacherous weapon in the hands of my memories. They build expectations and then watch as I deal with the consequences.

The half-open door that stands in front of me is not a colossal barrier. It is even seductive. And what is seduction if not the gradual accumulation of expectations? So, I acquiesce to the victor among the battling forces inside my mind. I push the door open and enter the room. I recognize at once the musty quality of the air. And as expected, on top of the small table lies the book that challenges the arrow of time.

#

The fact that the book lies open in front of me does not necessarily mean that I have to read it. The book has the perfect right to exist on its own. Inanimate as the book is, it has no will, no intentions. It cannot attempt to intersect my existence. First, I would have to read the words and extract a meaning from them. My interpretation would depend on my own experiences and, yet again, my expectations. Maybe the writer knew all along that I would be reading the book. Or maybe the writer did not care about the multiple interpretations people would give to the book. A more pressing question, why is this book inside this room all by itself?

Not remembering the origin of the book does not guarantee that I did not place it in this room myself. After all, this could be my house, and as such, I should have prior knowledge of the book. Likewise, I should have prior knowledge of my own origin, of the nature of the woman's chant, of my reasons for playing the flute. The lack of precise knowledge does not imply ignorance, nor does it imply forgetfulness. This may just be the essence of an irregular universe.

From what I already read in this book, time refuses to conform to a predictable and linear sequence of events. I wonder if the author experienced time in that manner, or whether he or she was trying to amuse the reader. Perhaps the author knew the book would be read in a totally different realm from where it was written. If that were the case, the author existed outside of time and had a clear intention. But intentions are useless because for them to be actualized, a series of circumstances would have to occur in some orchestrated synchronicity. And I am certain that entering this room this very moment relates to no preconceived plan.

I reach and grab the open book. I will be very careful not to turn a single page until I have read and interpreted the printed words in relation to my own temporal reality. But as I begin to focus on the first paragraph at the top of the page, I hear a few musical notes floating in the air. I close my eyes and remain expectant. One by one, the alluring notes enter the room and compose the melodious chant of the woman without expression. Unexpected, startling, extraordinary, the chant runs through me. This instant is of total luminosity. It goes on.

Caring not to alter the page where the book is open, I place it back on top of the small table. I am afraid of doing anything that would derail the course of time. I want to believe the chant is not a figment of my imagination. I want to believe that when I turn around, the expressionless face will be gazing at me. I want this instant to exist. I do not know exactly why I feel this way, but I do.

A sense of falling, a virtual vertigo is what arrives when I turn around and see the woman and her planar face standing still. I know she regards me with intensity, not because her eyes reveal anything special, but because she does not blink. The lips do not quiver, the forehead is at ease, and the little muscles controlling the eyelids are relaxed. There are no forces operating on her face—the frozen expression of an absence.

Her soft, uninterrupted voice levitates. I feel like touching the sound. Instead, I keep my hands next to me for fear of breaking the enchantment. Better to let the sound touch me. Inside of me, the chant explores the open and closed rooms of my mind. It sheds light on the shadows; it awakens forgotten memories. Whatever it discovers remains inside the rooms of my mind, for this chant has no echo. The movement of the forgotten earth is the vertigo I feel. And I wonder why this moment.

The woman walks past me. She takes the utmost care not to get too close. All along, she maintains her gaze fixed on me while continuing to chant. When she reaches the small table where the open book is witnessing all that occurs inside the room, she stops her chant. The melody, crashing against the walls, continues to reverberate until it exhausts itself completely. The woman then examines the book with much attention. I cannot tell what she reads or whether she relates to the book because her face reveals nothing. But after turning a few pages, she firmly closes the book and lays it on the table. Then the sun happens. Or perhaps I get the impression the sun happens. For a fraction of a second, I detect a smile on her face. But as soon as I become conscious of such smile, it vanishes, and her face assumes the previous expressionless quality. Maybe I projected that smile on her face. Or maybe she did smile after recognizing in the book the general uselessness of time.

With the same grace and care not to touch me, the woman makes her way to the door of the room. There she pauses and takes a long look at me. I am the one that smiles now, but she does not return the gesture. Once again, she begins to chant as she starts to walk down the corridor: the same melody, the same depth in her voice. The meaning, however, must be different. But if I were to construe a meaning, it would only be a reflection of my own needs and insecurities. I would feel as if I had touched the chant, but that would be false. I should just listen to the chant and let it be a chant. The chant, then, would be as naked as I am this moment. Without vestments, the chant and I contain the essence of what we are.

Now that the book is closed, I have no reason to remain in this room. Yes, I could just open the book to a random page and confront the alternative time. But that will likely create a sense of vertigo. I do not need vertigo at this moment. What I need is the certainty that following the chant down the corridor will bring me to her presence. Certainty, however, seems to have ceased to exist. In an attempt to assert some control of the unknown, I step out of the room and make sure the door is firmly closed and locked behind me. The book will remain closed inside this closed room. If this is my house, at some point, I will enter this room again.

The chant still exists, and I follow it. It trails away through the house in the direction of the kitchen. I follow it, imagining the woman has a desire for wine. Or perhaps that is another projection of mine, and the woman has no such desire. When I reach the entrance to the kitchen, I pause to listen. The melody she now sings is softer, meditative. I wonder if she is remembering a pleasant moment in the past. She could also be meditating about this instant. As I enter the kitchen, she stops singing at once. A silence now. An emptiness.

A naked man walking through a house in a quest for

a mysterious sound makes for a perfect quixotic image. Her silence probably makes sense considering the situation. But I cannot tell how she feels for there is no expression, nor is she singing anymore. I watch as she pours herself a glass of wine. She drinks from the glass with deliberate delicacy, as if she were savoring the instant. Without haste, I come to sit in front of her. She remains unperturbed, at least as observed from the outside. Then, she serves me a glass of wine and hands it to me. I take the glass and make sure not to touch her fingers by accident or by forethought.

After drinking some of the wine myself, I consider the possibility of talking to her. I could ask her so many questions. Who are you? Why are you in this place this moment? What is your chant about? The problem is that she may answer those questions, and as a result, bring a new reality into existence. She could also remain silent and allow for the potential of multiple realities to exist. There is danger in knowledge, as there is danger in ignorance. So, I say nothing and accept this moment as it is.

The woman breaks the silence with movement, but not with words. She reaches for my wooden flute, and, for a moment, I believe she will surprise me and start playing. However, she does not play a single note. Instead, she hands me the flute but does not make any gesture that would suggest for me to start playing. Furthermore, her vacuous eyes have no power to insinuate an action. It is my decision what to do with the flute and how to alter this instant.

I choose to play. Perhaps because I believe my music could speak to her, even though I do not know what to tell her. Or perhaps because she may respond to my music and reveal some of herself. Regardless of what may come about, I start playing the flute. The notes begin to rain on both of us. Loose notes, some of them lost notes. With no premeditated melody, the notes simply exist. When the first musical phrases emerge from the sonic nebula, I regard her expression with the hope of seeing the slightest change. But nothing on her face gives away an emotion.

The barren emotional landscape does not discourage me. I know she is listening to what I play, and somewhere inside of her, there is a response. I may never learn what that response is. Does it matter? Every single one of our actions impacts the perceptive reality of the world around us. Nevertheless, we carry on without knowing how the world responds to those intromissions. The responses may even lie dormant, unknown to those that harbor them. I may be responding now to an impact I experienced a long time ago. I may be playing this flute, not for this woman in front of me, but for another that instilled a response with palpable expression. And because I cannot attribute a clear origin to my musical phrases, I continue to play unbounded.

Once again, she initiates a movement, in response to the music, or maybe in response to her needs. She begins to walk away from me. After a few steps, she looks back. No smile, no tears. There she remains motionless. While still playing, I move closer to her. Her response is to take the same number of steps away from me. I feel like dropping the flute on the floor and rushing to touch her. But I do not do so. I focus instead on the melody emanating from the flute. It begins to change. These new notes may belong to another time, either before or after this time. They could have been hovering inside of me without me knowing. I let them flow and do as they will. Feeling free, then I try to get closer to her. And for the first time in quite a while, things happen in the way I had expected—the woman moves away from me.

The circle of fate has already been broken. And counting on the innumerable irregularities that rule this reality of mine, I play the flute even louder and continue to advance toward the woman. The space between us does not change, for she moves as I move, and her silence remains intact. Marching in tandem, we come across the strange abstract painting that once reflected her. I look into the painting's depth in search of myself. And once again, I do not find me—a duplicity of events that scares me deeply. The image of the woman begins to emerge in the same corner as it once did. But as I call her with my music, it vanishes into the shapeless shadows of the painting.

I reject causality. I cannot be the source of her motion. If she moves away, she moves away. If I approach her, I approach her. But one action does not imply the other. I could blame the music for creating this void between the two of us. Maybe the sonic matter pushes her away. To test this possibility, I stop blowing and remove the flute from my lips. The flute, however, continues to produce musical phrases with the same tonality and cadence as when I was playing. I recognize this as my music, perhaps played at some point in the past, or perhaps to be played in the future. I wonder if I am hearing this music in this now moment.

The woman, the music, and I continue to move through the corridors until we reach the front door of the house. She opens the door and a torrent of sunlight rushes in and bathes her immaculate face. I can see with clarity that no expression has settled on her face. She then looks out into the world. I wonder how she sees the world and if it seems as unreal as it seems to me. Determined, I take a few steps towards her. A mistake, apparently, for she crosses the door threshold and joins the world outside. As she vanishes away, I stand at the door with my two eyes open toward nothing.

#

The sunlight makes my naked body glow vigorously. I know I have the strength. To remain in this house is to accept the will of arbitrary gods. To venture out into the unknown is to will myself across an intemporal reality.

Then there is the emotional option to follow a yearning. However, I will not abide by the concept of choice at this moment. There is no sense in choosing anything for the selection process itself abrogates any preconceived outcome. I do get dressed, not out of embarrassment, but to avoid public harassment.

At the door, I vacillate. My mind tries to construct a narrative that could explain the vagaries of my evolving reality. But there is no apparent story like there is no apparent time. This, I feel, is the essence of freedom, an unfettered existence where the instances cannot be weaved together and the now is barely perceptible. Being born must be something like this. So, I step out to join the world and fill my lungs with air.

The sun insists on shining. I wonder if it is a content creature, the sun. Shedding light on everything must be incredibly satisfying, or a terrible curse. Maybe it does not stop shining because it cannot. That explains why the earth turns its face away from it on a nightly basis. Too intense, the sun. I try looking at it but cannot hold the stare. I understand the earth. Nevertheless, I can walk in its direction; I can follow the light.

The intense light gives rise to intense angular shadows. They try to hide, but the sun does not offer much opportunity. The shadows die the moment they are exposed, one-by-one, burnt away by the light. I have shadows inside my mind. I wonder what would happen if I expose them. Would they burn away, or would they hide even deeper? I may never know what is hidden in those shadows. Perhaps the shadows do not hide anything; instead, they safeguard thoughts until the appropriate light shines on them.

Under the sunlight, the houses don a different façade. What seems recognizable appears somewhat distorted. But distortion would imply a change from a known form. The problem is that nothing is exactly known to me, so the sense of distortion may be an illusion. A necessary illusion if I were to persist on trying to link this reality to a recognizable one. That exercise would destroy the sense of freedom I now feel and would obliterate my birth. Let the façades be as they wish.

I gather the warmth of the sunlight as it falls on my face. Every cell on my skin begins to vibrate more rapidly. I appreciate the sensation. With my eyes closed, all I see is a redness and a few floating shadows seeking refuge. This is not a reflection of what resides inside of me; this is only an illusion. This, however, may be what the sun divines about me. Even with its mighty light, the sun cannot see through me.

I follow the light. A light that travels from far away to land on my face. This does not make me a unique person, for the light shines on anyone and anything that happens to assume the right angle. If I were to march away from the light, the shadows would welcome me. But if I confront the light and march toward its source, the shadows will abandon me, and consequently, I will be exposed. An exposure that cannot hurt me because there is nothing to expose. Unless I were in the realm of the real, and that is still questionable.

The sunlight burns a path across the village with impunity. How free, the sun, to do as it wishes. This freedom attracts me. So, I continue on a march to where the light comes from. In so doing, I enter a latitude where the air feels somewhat compromised. A putrid smell begins to slip into my reality, and I wonder if the wound is somewhere near. And the further I pursue the sunlight, the thicker the miasma becomes. In this realm, not even the sunlight can dissuade the air molecules from aggregating and concocting such a fetidness.

This is not a moment but an era. This is not me but the whole of humankind. This is when we feel we can make a decision and change the course of events, or when we allow for what needs to happen, happen anyway. This is when I need to confront the turbulence of this instant and become aware of the instability of human affairs. This is when I question Tyche, the blind mistress of Fortune, how to proceed. The answer, unheard but understood, is to do nothing—for there is nothing that can be done.

I decide not to decide anything but to continue following the sunlight. And with every step, the certainty of the wound becomes more evident. Soon I reach a crossroad, at which point the stench comes charging at me like a freight train. It enters through my nose and floods my lungs. At the same time, an oblique sun ray enters through my eyes and lodges itself in my forebrain. Assaulted by the elements, I can barely walk straight. I pause and wait for the instant to burn out and vanish away. Once in the clear, I come to terms with the reality that becomes manifest in front of me. The wound, pestilent and divisive, extends from left to right as far as I can see and blocks my passage. I can retreat and pretend the wound does not exist. But who am I to deny an existence?

The wound does not bleed for me. It does not take me into consideration. Its cells will continue to stink regardless of my reactions. It will continue to ooze its decay. I am immaterial to the wound, and perhaps to the world on this side of the wound. I realize that what lies in front of me is not a wall, nor an abyss, but a state of mind. The wound is the rupture of our expectations.

Without hope, without desire, without regret, I advance toward the wound. I cannot tell if I am falling into it or climbing over it. I cannot tell if I am inside the wound. All I can tell is that I feel nothing as if a deep vacuum has swallowed me and everything around me is a void. This instant turns into a century, or perhaps it has taken me a century to reach this instant.

Part Four:

TOWARD THE LIGHT

When I open my eyes, I find myself at the edge of the sidewalk. There is a certain clarity in the air imparting a suspicious legitimacy to this moment. The street in front of me is perfectly straight, and the houses are meticulously aligned. I know exactly where I am for everything is utterly recognizable. The sun is directly above my head and I cast no shadow. In 60 seconds, it will be 12:01 pm. I have no doubts about that. I could convince myself that a grand disorder is about to overtake me. But that would be a lie.

I look around for the man whose eyes were cascading. He is nowhere. At least, he is not here at this moment, which I find completely understandable. I do not feel responsible for him. He has his reality and I have mine. This is mine, as real as it is expected.

With determination, I walk in the direction of the music hall where I will perform a concert starting at 1:00 pm. The piece I will play is very clear in my mind. I can see the notes, the silences. Nothing is left to chance or improvisation. Plus, arriving at the music hall ahead of time will give me the opportunity to practice the most difficult passages. There will be no mistakes. I can almost guarantee that.

On my way to the music hall, I stop at my favorite bistro, where the waitress has already placed a glass of my favorite wine at my usual table. She knows I will not stay too long. She also knows the days when I play at the music hall. I do not talk to her about any other aspects of my life for fear that she may show interest. In reality, all I am doing is completing the habitual circle to fend off potential uncertainties.

Once inside the music hall, I feel the calmness descending on me. This is my ambit, my zone of musical comfort. This is where the expected comes to be. My flute waits for me in my locker, anxious to be played. I then join the other members of the ensemble, and we rehearse together. Everyone knows their part to perfection. When I get out on the stage, I will bring the sheet music with me. We all do. Not because we do not remember the music, but just in case we forget.

As expected, the concert begins on time. We perform with finesse, and our sound is sublime. All the notes are played as written. The audience seems pleased for they applaud abundantly. For the encore, we play two additional pieces to satiate their enthusiasm. This is what I expect when I play a concert—a perfect control of the music.

I bring the flute with me on the way back to my house. But I must stop at the bistro, once more, to let the waitress know the concert turned out as I anticipated. When she sees me go through the door, she rushes to serve me a glass of my wine. This is exactly how it happened the previous time I played, as well as multiple times before that. I think she already knows what to presume. There are no hidden demands in our exchange. This is just the natural order of things.

On the street, people greet me. They call me by my name and wish me well. They seem honestly happy to come upon my presence. Guarding their respective posts, these soldiers of regular life flank the length of the sidewalk from the music hall all the way to my house. Rarely does a person change. And when that happens, I become acquainted with the new person at once. There is a white cat that lives in the house at the corner of this street. When he hears me approaching, he steps on the sideway and offers me his belly. He gets the petting he demands. He always does.

Once in front of my house, I pause to contemplate its formal beauty. The symmetry and the elegant proportions of the facade make this house a comfortable place to be. Then there is the number "3" to guarantee the best of luck. Many things have happened in this house. I could trace the trajectory of interconnected events that have occurred in my past. They make me what I am today, and this house has been the witness.

I enter my house like I enter the realm of the known, where surprises are replaced by certainties, and the air is crisp and easy to breathe. Once inside, the first order of things is to pour myself another glass of wine. The rest of the afternoon will progress as it should. After placing the flute in the music room, where it will rest unperturbed as instruments tend to do, I make my way to the patio for further contemplation of this ambit of mine. No place is better than this patio for reflection. Here the wind comes at its own discretion, and the flowers are prone to agree with my ideas. There are no opposing forces, except when it rains. Then I just go back inside the house and watch the water droplets in free fall.

After having some of the wine, my first consideration relates to the sense of emptiness that continues to hover over me. This emptiness has been growing little by little until its presence can no longer be denied. This emptiness is mine. There is no doubt about that. But I fail to understand where it comes from and what it means. It is different from a void, in the sense that a void has a place in the world. This emptiness can only exist inside my mind and lacks a physical presence. And it cannot be an absence, for an absence implies a previous presence that is no longer there. Perhaps emptiness has no meaning; it simply is.

A series of interconnected temporal, biological, and physical events have taken place to bring me to this seating position, in this patio, this very instant. How else could my reality be explained? I surrender to this instant, believing that it owes its existence to its predecessors, a long line of other instants that have already existed. I am one in the line of many. The wave started when the world was created, and now is cresting over me. There is the night, and there is the day. They take turns and never trample each other. I take comfort in such rhythm. When I abandon consciousness, it always finds me at the other end of the night. Like a well-crafted sonata, all the movements of the world have a reason to be and eventually coalesce. There is nothing to fear.

However, the wine seems to dislodge something inside my mind because the shadow of a doubt emerges. I can see its profile but not its face. When I try to uncover the doubt, it hides. I never knew about the existence of this doubt. It may have been lurking in the forsaken rooms of my mind for a long time. But the problem is that I do not know the nature of the doubt. What is the doubt about, what is it that is not clear?

Enough. This is not the moment for discomfort. I better get up and approach the flowers. I consider their colors and shapes. I marvel at their fragility. I watch as the petals frolic in the wind. They are happy to exist in this patio as the flowers that they are. And I am content to share this patio with them. The earth sustains them; the water gives them life. They have a clear place in this universe.

Drinking the last drop of wine could be considered a tragedy. To prevent unnecessary malaise, I part with the flowers and venture into the kitchen where more wine is surely available. The reason for drinking my favorite wine is precisely to eradicate the possibility of drinking a less agreeable one. It is not only for the pleasure the wine gives me but for safety. I pour another glass, but the moment I bring it to my lips, an uncomfortable thought pierces my awareness. What if the wine irks that unsavory doubt once more? What if the doubt gets out from the shadows and shows its face in broad daylight? Maybe the wine is not my friend. That would be another tragedy.

The emptiness I have been sensing comes to sit next to me. I regard it with the utmost attention, but there is nothing to see. This sensation is immaterial, which does not mean that it is unreal, just that it is not composed of molecules like my body, or the wine itself. A sensation can weigh more than an elephant and occupy an even larger space. It is immense, this emptiness.

I suppose the emptiness serves to proclaim that something is not there. But I cannot imagine what it is that is not there. When I look around me, everything seems to be where it should. I have no material yearnings. This house of mine contains all I ever wanted, and most of the unwanted items have already been discarded. Nothing is missing, and everything inside this house has a reason to exist.

As for my past, I may not recall it in its entirety, but I am certain its force has been accounted for. All the previous events in my life have been interweaved to form a lineal history bringing me to this very instant. There are no missing or unaccounted moments. I owe my present life to my past. And this present is the platform from where my future will spring.

In music, I feel complete. I have played all the meaningful concerts with grace and clarity. There may be notes between the notes but those are irrelevant. My flute seems content when I play it. The applause confirms my sense of mastery, and so does the waitress at the bistro. I do not compose music. That is for the gods. I am more real than that.

In spite of all I know and control in this ambit of mine, the sense of emptiness grabs me by the neck and threatens to suffocate me. I can pretend to ignore its existence. But in its disincarnate substantiality, this emptiness is more real than air itself. I do not know what it wants from me, nor for how long will it haunt me. Perhaps this is the way I will feel for the rest of my life. That is not an acceptable thought.

The glass of wine has not abandoned me. I appreciate its company and proceed to commune with its soul. I am aware of the inherent risk but need the soothing right now. As expected, my heart rate settles at a comfortable level. I then close my eyes and concentrate on the tannic notes of the wine. I try to eviscerate my mind from all worries and concerns. I try to take comfort in the concept that reality is constructed out of my perceptions and my very own life—nothing else. But as it already happened in the patio, the shadow of a doubt materializes. Even in its nebulous form, the prospect of such doubt terrifies me. I abhor looking directly at the doubt for fear that it will look directly at me. Then what would I do? Perhaps the doubt is nothing but a dream that refuses to vanish in daylight. Should I explore what is the substance of this doubt? I would like to know what there is to doubt. But if I do, I may need to confront that baselessness of something I feel sure about. I wonder how dangerous that would be.

What I feel sure about is that this world is determined by a scaffolding of truths and consequences operating over time. That sense of certainty is the blood of my life. To entertain any other possibility, whether by doubt or violent confrontation, would be like slicing my veins. I would bleed to death. Irrelevant doubts, those about menial details in life, do not frighten me. But to question determinism is like facing the wrath of a sun.

This sense of imbalance forces me to forgo wine for the rest of the day. Tiptoeing over the edge of an abyss goes against my nature. I flee the kitchen and look for refuge in my reading room, where books offer the truce I need. I feel safe among these bounded dreams. I have come to realize that the existence of a book of fiction is a wondrous feat. What are the chances that a herd of words would coalesce on the page in such an order to express the inner feelings of invented lives, to describe places that never existed, to make me see what I never imagined? And if a book delivered me beyond myself?

I pick up the book I have yet to finish. It reveals the future of a man as events he had already experienced in his own past, a sort of time mirror. As I turn the pages, my mind settles, and I find a certain peace. The relationship between the narrator and myself is as intense and emotionally complex as any relationship I ever had with another human being. The slow accumulation of the soul of the other, a satisfying human need, occurs in the turning of pages and the deciphering of life as rendered by the prose. This novel provides an intercourse with selves, albeit imagined, but just as real. The author creates an image of himself and another image of myself; he makes me, as he makes his second self. And I enjoy this beautiful intimacy. But the peace provided by the reading proves to be short-lived, for the profile of the doubt comes to light once more.

What if there was another world, fictional, perhaps imaginary? And if that world was real? Then the universe would not be regular, and it could be conceived of as having alternating layers of causality and chaos. I try to turn my eyes away, but the penetrating gaze of the doubt burns through me. What if all that ever occurred to me, those interweaved lines of causality that I believe in, were nothing but accidents caused by chance? A sense of discomfort floods me. I feel lightheaded. This doubt unsettles my historical, cultural, and psychological assumptions. This doubt dismantles the consistency of my tastes, values, memories… It grows inside of me like a fungus. It forces its way past my resistance and reaches the confines of my mind. This doubt highjacks the logical machinery and brings it to a halt.

In the midst of the struggle to keep my reality from

collapsing, I take a measure of myself. I find no defi-
cits. The doubt was the only thing missing. Once it has
wedged itself into my consciousness, I realize that all
of me seems to be present. Furthermore, now that the
doubt exists, the sense of emptiness is no longer. Intact
and inspired, I cannot do otherwise than seek still further.

#

I come to realize the world is not composed of parallel lines intersecting infinite sets of other parallel lines.
Right angles do not exist in nature; we force them upon
it. Unbeknownst to me, it is possible that my relationship with reality has always been an oblique one. Indeed, there may not be any life worth living which is not
consciously oblique. If I were to respect the reality of the
world, I am afraid that I can only approach such reality
by incidental means. My path ought to be an oblique
one.

I bolt out of my house into the streets I may have
falsely believed I know so well. By questioning any apparent sense of knowledge, I invite a legion of doubts.
Gradually, then, the emptiness is filled by the abundance
of doubts and questions. There is a certain sweetness in
not knowing, like a nectar, ambrosia, perhaps.

The man whose eyes were cascading had already seen
this truth. That is why no hands were there to collect his

eyes. He had no need for them. He must be nearby. I may find him just around the corner. In front of him, I will find the street I ought to cross. However, I do not need to find him to know where that street is located. All I have to do is follow an oblique path and expect nothing.

Unaccustomed to operating in such a fragile scheme, an avalanche of doubts about my whereabouts and that of the street befalls me. There is that sweetness again. I make a strong effort not to assert control over the path to follow. Old habits and reassuring expectations want to tie me down to my habitual rational ways. They attempt to dissipate all possible doubts. But the sweetness is more powerful. Ignoring the street signs and the sense of direction, I walk obliquely toward nowhere.

While drunk on the ambrosia of doubts, the sense of time loses its grip on me. Walking timelessly is utterly liberating. One instant follows another without force or pressure. I begin to understand that measuring time is just a working hypothesis. Who are we to measure immutable or permanent time? How do we know when time begins or when it ends?

At some point, this improbable trajectory brings me to the very street I may have crossed before. There is no man with eyes cascading or any other person around me. I find myself at the center of this instant that feels totally personal. Could I be completely alone? I cannot tell, but I welcome the doubt. The entire universe may reside inside of me. At the same time, I may be nothing to the universe, only the concept of an unconfirmed existence. And as such, I regard the full length of the street in front of me and marvel at its obliqueness.

This time I close my eyes. I do not need them to see the street. I can sense the pulsating flow of people, of automobiles. I can sense the channeled anxiety dividing two realities I have yet to reconcile. I am not afraid of crossing the street with my eyes closed. Let the crossing happen as it will, without any effort to direct my steps. As long as I traverse the street in an angle, I trust that I will reach the other side.

My first step finds a solid ground that does not give under the weight of my body. A few more steps and the bony labyrinth in my inner ear sends a signal of terror. I stand still for a moment until the sense of balance comes back to me. Once stable, I venture into the middle of the street. The pulsating flow gathers strength. I feel it all around me. But nothing runs me over. The fact that the expected massacre of my body does not materialize confirms my suspicion that the reality I am about to enter bears no resemblance with the reality I am leaving behind. And this awakening is not necessarily joyous, but radically liberating.

The other side of the street receives me without pomp or circumstance. There is no applause, no homage to my crossing. When I look around for witnesses, there is nobody to be found. I am aware that I crossed the street. I did not watch myself in the process of crossing, and apparently, no one else did. But I know I went through a threshold. Is that threshold located in the physical world, or does it exist only in my mind? Does it matter?

The physicality of my crossing becomes manifest when the penetrating smell of decaying flesh assaults me. I have smelled homelessness before, sad and re-volting, but this stench is much stronger. When I turn around to look at the street I think I just crossed; it has disappeared. What I find instead is an oblique laceration exposing putrid flesh. This is a deep and unfathomable wound that apparently refuses to heal. I cannot imagine the cause of this injury, nor when it occurred. It may be an old wound seriously aggravated at this moment.

Leaving the wound behind seems natural to me. I cannot heal it. And I cannot bear smelling it any longer. So, I turn toward the village in front of me and open my mind to all possibilities, especially the unexpected ones. In this instant, nothing is clear, and nothing is partic-ularly obscure either. Shadows and light take turns leading me through the village until I reach a peaceful square planted with leafy trees. I could walk around the edge of the square while admiring the quivering leaves. But the era of right angles has come to an end, so I follow the path that cuts through the square from one corner to another, diagonally.

In this moment, I refuse any mission. With no need to accomplish anything, my only obligation is to exist. In existing, I have already accomplished all that falls under my control. And the reality around me seems to be in agreement with me. Recognizable, but indefinite at the same time, this reality takes me by the hand and welcomes my presence. I simply glide along and enjoy the freedom.

The concept of time takes a stab at me. It wants to force its way into my considerations. I could easily yield to this temptation because of its promising structure. What comes before leads to what follows after. But that arrow has been broken. I do not know "when" that happened, which makes sense because knowing the "when" would imply that the arrow had not been broken. Besides, we count time when we have nothing better to count.

The instant then expands and encompasses everything in this semi-familiar reality. I feel like myself, or a version of myself. The fact that I cannot tell what version of myself is active this moment is proof that there is no way to know—this, a liberating thought that breaks the chains of habitual expectations. I sense the natural order of things losing its grip on me, perhaps because it is not natural for things to have such an order. Therefore, in this instant, I walk as myself, and the reason or veracity of that proposition is of no consequence.

By placing one foot in front of the other, I move ahead while the world does its own turning below my feet. With the help of the spinning world, I must be traveling very fast. I do not feel the speed of our concomitant movements, the world and me, but I know it is real as it is real that my skin feels the wind which I cannot see. My steps are meager when compared to the physicality of these invisible and powerful forces. And as such, step by step, I come to stand in front of the number "3" I easily recognize.

This is the house that could be my house. This is the house from where I left at some point in a time indistinct. The house lacks the capacity to displace itself, so any doubts about its existence originate outside of the house, in my mind, or elsewhere, in this reality or in another. At first, I am inclined to let myself impetuously into the house. But that would be the natural order of things, an order that is now suspect. So, in the spirit of a missionless moment, I refrain from taking another step and simply stand in front of the house. As I contemplate the house from the outside, a few memories claim admittance into my mind. I refuse to acknowledge them, for they may contaminate the purity of not knowing what version of myself is doing the contemplation. I am free to stand here in this very instant and accomplish nothing. I take comfort in knowing that without taking a single step, the world is taking me around the universe.

The front window frames an interior vision of the house. The temptation is to watch until something revealing appears. A revelation that I am not necessarily searching since I am content with my missionless travel. But the temptation does not ask permission to exert its force; it simply bears its weight. Thus, I watch without wanting to watch and accept the consequences.

The window frame is full of nothing. There are only shadows and the color gray. It does not mean that the house contains a void inside. It probably means that the window opens into a vague area of the house occupied only by air at this moment. Having been inside this house, as I suppose I have, I can attest that it contains objects, very few memories, and maybe even wine. The only way to explain the dearth of visions is to believe the window is withholding something from me. But why would a window, whose nature is essentially an absence, want to withhold anything?

A shadow, then, begins to form at the very edge of the frame. At first, it behaves as if its nature is a liquid one. But then it solidifies by assuming the shape of a body. Not a body in its entirety, because the frame seems to be absconding half of it. I can only distinguish what appears to be a head and a shoulder. The shadow does not move, and I decide to remain just as motionless. I wonder if that head contains two eyes and if those eyes are staring at me. Do those eyes see me as a shadow? Do those eyes know who I am?

The shadow abandons the edge of the frame and reveals its full profile. What I see is the unequivocal shape of a woman occupying the center of the frame. And, once again, it assumes a static position as if wanting to see me very well or wanting to be seen by me. The temptation is to watch until the identity of the woman is somehow revealed. That temptation, however, may be nothing other than a misplaced hope. The hope that in making such a recognition, I would feel grounded. But how could I be grounded if the world is turning and turning under my feet?

When bored or completely satisfied, I cannot tell, the shadow departs from the frame. Only the color gray remains visible through the window. This must be the nature of an absence, a framed window inside of which the color gray reigns supreme. But for an absence to exist, a former presence is necessary, even if that presence is nothing but a shadow. Time, then, is an integral part of the process because only in following a presence, could an absence occur. So, by discarding time and its oppressive insistence, this new reality would be free from absences. This now-instant is the only presence that concerns me.

I struggle not to enter the house. The force of inquiry, that ancient need to know more than we should, threatens to make me act in preconceived ways. The fact that the house looks familiar and that the shadow of a woman reaches out to me through the window frame would have been enough to unleash a natural order of events—an inquiry. The expected has run its course already and brought me nothing but disillusions. To yield to the natural order of things is to succumb under the weight of a failed reality. But by resisting, would I not be following the expected course of denial, just as natural as any other order. By struggling against a deep-seated desire, I would be one among a legion of rebels who march along a very well-paved road.

Perhaps there is nothing to do. What would happen if I were to push aside all illusory decision processes? I could attempt not to pursue and not to resist at the same time. The now-instant will then emerge in its full presence. And the reality of this instant will be in itself imminent. That is a sense of freedom I have yet to savor fully. I start to realize I have been imprisoned by that pestilent wound without knowing the extent of its wretchedness.

Thus, I close my eyes and detach from all sensorial input. I eviscerate my mind from preconceptions and expectations. As for my memories, it takes little effort to eradicate them, for they are thin as silk. By not moving, I move. By not thinking, I obtain knowledge. By not wanting, I receive. I open my hands and let go of the reins. All I need to know is that the world continues to turn under my feet. And it turns indeed, for I am no longer in the same place I was before. I cannot see the voyage while my eyes are closed, but I can feel a displacement—displacement that may be interior and exterior at the same time.

A second or an epoch must have elapsed. I am not certain. The earth must have undergone multiple revolutions around itself. I cannot tell. But when the air comes to embrace me, awakening all my senses, I find myself in the middle of a patio where flowers dare. This patio speaks to me. Not with a human voice, but with the voice of reason. It tells me to be free. I find the message completely reasonable. The patio does not offer further details, for it has provided what a patio can provide—openness and a sense of freedom.

#

I could look back to where I came from, to a time before this time. What a futile exercise that would be. This instant exists on its own and bears no relation to any other instant before or after. This house receives me as if I were coming from elsewhere, but I may be coming from nowhere other than this house. The only bandit that can rob me of my freedom is myself. And there is no sense in running away from myself, as there is no sense in trying to find me in a place away from this house or in time distinct from this very instant.

The only reasonable recourse is to float and allow. With an open mind, the face of reality will reveal itself to me. Even if that reality were to appear questionable, I would accept it as my own. Perhaps not even as my own, for who am I to claim ownership of any measure of reality? And the more I try to encapsulate the nature of this instant, the more I realize the capsule is essentially permeable.

However, I cannot ignore that behind those French doors, there is the rest of the house. And what allures me more than anything else are the shadows that inhabit the house. They may be corporeal, in which case, I am casting some of them. And, so would a woman whose presence eludes me thus far. But if the shadows were cast by non-corporeal entities, I would have to explore deep into my senses. Hunting for shadows may prove a dangerous enterprise.

Still floating, I allow. My feet remain motionless while the earth continues to turn—my body, a sail that responds to the wind. I am being displaced by the natural order of elements and not by those of the mind. The wind steers me through the French doors into the heart of the house that could be my house. Once the wind returns to the freedom of the patio, I am left standing on my own two feet in the middle of a wide corridor. Around me, there are multiple objects casting angular and round shadows. And then there are shadows that pertain to no observable object. Those intrigue me the most.

A shadow is nothing but the absence of light. The difference between a temporal presence and its subsequent absence—the kind we experience when a person dies—and that of the shadow and light, is that for the shadow to exist, the light needs to exist at the same time. A shadow owes its nature as an absence to the simultaneous presence of light. I now comprehend that the shadow of the woman at the window frame implies the light of the woman.

I could search for the light inherent to the woman. I could try to eradicate the shadows that surround me. I could pretend I have control over their dialectical opposition. My will, however, is virtually nonexistent. Not as a result of weakness or boredom, but because I come to realize that purposefulness is only apparent. The wide corridor will host me, with its angular shadows and oblique lights, and will allow me to satiate my need to exist in this very instant.

And by not wanting to see, I come to see an abstract painting hanging on the wall of the corridor. A painting I feel I have seen before but is now unrecognizable due to the transmuting nature of its colors and nebulous shapes. I may have been born out of this painting, or I may have died into it. Somehow, it seems to commune with my nature even when my nature is unclear to me. When I look into the painting, a sense of vertigo overwhelms me, and my feet lose contact with the ground. I fall into the consciousness of the painting. And in this vast space, there are no shadows, only air, and colors.

Unanchored, I revolve inside the immeasurable space. I reach with my arms to find the confines of the space and touch nothing. The space that now contains me is not contained by any frontier. I am surrounded by a consciousness beyond my own. And that is how my limits disappear for they are no longer necessary. In the pure now, there are no limits. There were hard limits on the other side of the fetid wound, imposed by centuries of expectations. Perhaps those limits never existed, and what I touched were arbitrary constructs of an ill-conceived reality.

The air begins to move around me. I can hear it. It vibrates, attaining a sonorous quality I barely recognize. This is not the sound of the earth spinning but a vocal expression of a wish. As the vocalization grows more and more organized, it becomes evident to me that it comes from a woman chanting. I quiet my mind and open my senses. I dismantle my external barriers. Only then do I feel a presence other than my own presence. In the midst of this extended consciousness, there appears to be an "other."

Unheralded by shadows, for only colors surround me, the light of a woman is born. And as the light pours into my instant, it ushers in the melodious chant, a chant that emanates from the lips of a woman, a woman whose lips reveal no palpable emotion. I observe the rest of her face, lunar in its whiteness, impassive. This is the woman whose light created the shadows I saw through the window frame. How probable is this woman? As probable as light, perhaps.

Inside this house, inside this painting, inside myself, I find the grandest exteriority and freedom. All the layers of causality and chaos become diaphanous. As I revolve inside this space, time disintegrates. Everything that ever has been and ever will be is contained within this instant. In this reality, I accept the improbable, for the probable owes itself to a defunct order. Floating adrift I regard the luminous expression in the woman's face. And I understand that we are not, but we are.

Jorge Armenteros was born in Cuba, his family leaving for Madrid, Spain, then Tampa, Florida, before finally settling in Puerto Rico. After graduating cum laude from Harvard University, he acquired an MD at the University of Puerto Rico, an MA in Spanish and Latin American Literature at New York University, and an MFA in Creative Writing at Lesley University. Armenteros is the author of the 2015 International Latino Book Award winner *The Book of I* (Jaded Ibis Press), and *The Striped Tunic Trilogy* (Spuyten Duyvil Press). Armenteros resides in the South of France.